Jacob's Daughter

Jacob's Daughter

Naomi Williams

HARBOR
HOUSE

Jacob's Daughter
By Naomi Williams
A Harbor House Book/2007

Copyright 2007 by Naomi Williams

For information address:
HARBOR HOUSE
111 TENTH STREET
AUGUSTA, GA 30901

Jacket and book design by Nathan Elliott
ISBN: 978-1-891799-80-8

Library of Congress Cataloging-in-Publication Data is available on the
Library of Congress Web site.

Printed in the United States of America
10 9 8 7 6 5 4 3 2 1

For my sister, Bernice, who opened

Books to her younger sibling

And unfolded the mystery and

Magic of words;

And

For my niece, Vivian, whose

Faith in and love for me

Have sustained me through

The years.

And his soul clave unto Dinah

The daughter of Jacob, and

He loved the damsel, and spake

Kindly unto the damsel.

—Genesis 34:3

Acknowledgements

Five years have passed since *Two Rivers*. Again I am grateful to Harbor House for making publication possible. I also owe great gratitude to my friends, Lynn Mertins, Deborah Jones, and Evelyn Wilkinson, for proofing and advice. My appreciation goes to Nathan Elliott who designed the cover. To my editor, Peggy Cheney, and also my former student, I am most indebted for her expertise. Without her, publication would not have been possible. Thanks are in order to a star student. It is she who synthesized themes in *Jacob's Daughter* for an appropriate cover.

PROLOGUE

After eight hours in labor, Anna delivered her seventh child, but not "trailing clouds of glory," Wordsworth's poetic description of birth. Instead came forth a scrawny, wrinkled five-pound girl—all bones and no flesh—a miniature scarecrow without clothes. What was even odder about her advent was the absence of the lusty cry. Dr. Johnson shook his fat, bald head and pronounced her dead. Grandma Jernigan declared it a blessing and called her "such an ugly little thing." Anna screamed, "God's punishing me. I didn't want her. I tried to get rid of her. I've had my share of younguns—six to the time and two miscarriages. It's your entire fault, Jacob. You men ain't never satisfied."

"Hush, Mama," Jacob soothed. His large stubby fingers gently pushed her damp black hair from her forehead as he leaned down to kiss her. "Tut, tut." These were his special words saved to turn torrents into still waters. "It's all in God's hands. His will is done," he mumbled brokenly.

But not quite. Over by the chimney fat Aunt Phoenix, ballooned in her white midwifery, turned the "ugly little thing" over her aproned knee. She had been delivering babies in Mount Tabor when Dr. Johnson was in knee britches and had earned the name Aunt as a title of respect accorded to colored folks upon whom their white neighbors relied. Her experienced black hand, soft but strong as any field hand, smacked the baby's back smartly. A strange quiet invaded the room. Time stood still. Jacob would say later, "It was just like old Joshua in the Bible. He commanded the sun to stand still for a whole day." But now came an eerie sound, a ghost of a whimper—a pitiful protest registering reluctance to enter an alien world.

"Lord, Gawd, Miss Anna. She done come alive." The old woman turned the scrawny mass of skin, bone, and slime, mumbling mumbo jumbo words to slits revealing a line of brown eyes. The proverbial cry of newborns shaped on the tiny puckered mouth evoked a bleat like that of a calf abandoned by its mother. Aunt Phoenix's capable black hands held the baby cradle fashion as her keen eyes scrutinized through folds of flesh. Rising from the glowing embers winking through gray ashes on the hearth, Aunt Phoenix reached for the cotton blanket and swaddled the newborn. Thus the voice of one, born in slavery and mature in wisdom through adversity, pronounced the prognosis. "Ain't no idiot child here. She gon have pretty brown eyes. Look how she walling them. That little pea brain done working."

"Give her to me, Aunt Phoenix." Jacob stretched out his arms. "This child is a miracle. Raised from the dead. Mama, we got to name her something special. A Bible name. DeBorah." He would accent the *BOR* until Deborah, reading the book of Judges at the age of four, would correct her father's antiquated pronunciation. "She was a great judge," he continued. "And she lived near Mount Tabor, too. God has spoken this day," he proclaimed solemnly.

He handed his new daughter back to Aunt Phoenix, who eased her to her mother's bosom. "She won't take it," Anna wailed as the little mouth rejected the brown nipple. "She'll die for sure if she don't eat." Her voice twinned hope and fear.

In the meantime, Jacob Jernigan had brought from across

the hall the family Bible from its place of prominence on the shelf of a black mahogany table centering the parlor. Opening it to the pages between the Old and New Testaments, he recorded in black ink in a flourish of curlicue letters: Deborah Jernigan, April 14, 1928. "It's Easter Sunday," he said, closing the book as the grandfather clock struck midnight; and because he belonged to the Masonic Order, he concluded solemnly, "So mote it be," the ritual ending of the prayer sacred to members of the fraternal organization as old as the Knight Templars. As he moved toward the parlor to replace the frayed leather book, he missed the quizzical look of brown eyes asking, "What did you say?"

CHAPTER

One

HOME SCHOOLING

F rom the beginning Deborah observed many rituals. She watched the family gather nightly around the chimney bringing their Bibles for devotions. Mama's lap and hands were occupied with Deborah, whom she folded in blankets even in July lest the baby get another cold and develop pneumonia. In a strong, clear, and precise voice, never stumbling over a word, Hannah, the oldest, read first. When Belle's turn came, Hannah would smile superciliously at her younger sister who could not care less whether she pronounced *verily* correctly or whether she changed the accent to sound like the name of a colored girl picking cotton. What interested Belle most was how boys looked at her as she swished into church each Sunday, tossing her jet-black tresses and rolling her eyes to tally how many swains eyed her. She was, indeed, the belle of Mount Tabor. Mama called her the most beautiful child she had and reminded Jacob that she herself had looked just like that when he had brought her from Horry County and before she had been broken down with child-bearing. Belle's place around the hearth was abruptly vacated when she sneaked out of church one Sunday to join Bennie Burton, twice her age, to fly off in his Ford to find a Justice of the Peace. Her younger brother, William, swore manfully that he would kill the thief that had stolen his sister. Anna screamed that Belle would die having children before she was sixteen. Jacob patted her head with "Tut, tut" and left the dilemma in God's hands. Belle's exit fell hard upon Hannah. Like the Biblical customs, it was expected that the eldest marry first. So Hannah found John Martin, who had neither land nor prospects, but who was willing to make Hannah, plain but intelligent, a bride. Ten-year-old Lily, when her turn came to read the Holy Writ, punctuated the verses with "Praise gods and amens." Lily had already been baptized in Chapel Creek and gave testimony to her faith at revival twice a year.

Of all her siblings Deborah liked Beryl best. Years later, Deborah would learn the origin of her name, but as early as she could remember Beryl was a gem. It was Beryl who carved castles in grits and peopled them with ham and eggs and told such stories that Deborah, agape at the wonder of frogs turning into princes, would hardly notice a spoonful of a demolished turret sliding down her throat. It was Beryl who read to her *A Child's Bible Stories*, tales from the Brothers Grimm, or *A Child's Garden of Verse*. She always elicited the promise of such a session only after Deborah had eaten her supper. Thus tales from the holy book and books not so holy put flesh on the scrawny frame which did not magically grow into a beautiful Belle, but at least Grandma Jernigan dropped the "such an ugly little thing" and claimed credit for the transformation due to her sugar tits.

Undoubtedly Hannah—in love with new words from the dictionary—must have named Gamin, six years Deborah's senior. He was a mischievous little boy who lived up to his name and who might have been lovable if a streak of meanness had not crept in during his tenure as the spoiled brat that Anna hoped would be

14

her last. Hannah, like the rest, endured Gamin's temper and kicks in the shins but prided herself that she had had the prescience to give her little brother such an apt name. She would also remind Deborah frequently that only she, Hannah, had made three grades in one year. Deborah disliked her almost as much, but not quite so much as she disliked Gamin, who pulled her hair when no one was looking and who threatened to smash her dolls. For one thing Hannah could pronounce the name Deborah correctly and beautifully, although she resented the impersonal "sister" by which Hannah addressed her.

The two brothers, modern Cain and Abel, ate at the same table, slept in the same bed, and received the same strap for fighting. William, the older, far more trustworthy than his male sibling, smarted under the lash more frequently, taking the blame for Gamin's shenanigans, a bitter memory to be carried into adulthood. Deborah, favoring the gentle William, longed to see the day when she could trip Gamin's long legs or smash his devilish blue eyes with a ripe tomato, settling scores for her and William.

Deborah's birth also brought another resident into the household, Ginger Snap Leggett, a dark-skinned sixteen-year-old nanny with flashing black eyes and a laugh that started somewhere deep inside and came out in blasts of bubbles so big that even Daddy at his sternest could not restrain a smile. She was a practical joker, a mischief-maker, and the surrogate mother for Deborah. Not demonstrative with family members, Deborah in Ginger Snap's lap would throw her arms around Ginger Snap's neck and attempt to lavish kisses until Mama stopped her with "No, you don't kiss colored people." Ginger Snap, who was not in the least sensitive and had never heard the word *racism* or *discrimination*, would let out a belly laugh with "Why, Miss Anna, I taste just like your ginger snaps. My Ma said I come here snappy and full of ginger. I gonna make this chile big and fat. 'Fore long, she be outrunning you." Before long Deborah had dropped the Snap, deciding Ginger a more appropriate appellate for her idol.

And so it was. It was Ginger's strong hands that guided her

15

when she, almost three, took her first steps. It was Ginger who introduced her to molasses and cornbread eaten sitting on a bench around a rough-hewn pine table with Delia's eight children, all under ten years. "Ginger," Deborah questioned, "how come Delia's house smells different from ours?"

"Cause the good Lord, when he made us, cleaned out all you white folk's stink." The inevitable laugh followed and Deborah's knowledge and love of African lore grew. It was Ginger who prayed over Deborah's plate and bribed her to eat: "Do Lord, send this good chile a piece of candy." Magically a Mary Jane would be dropped from on high straight into Deborah's empty plate. Rich laughter gurgled from her brown throat as her strong arms gave Deborah a squeeze.

One day Ginger carried her charge to Jerusalem, the African Methodist Episcopal Church in the heart of Little Hamlet. Years later, Deborah would wonder if the name of the colored settlement had been labeled by a white supremacist drawing from Ham in the Bible, who looked on his father's nakedness and who, with all his descendents, was, therefore, cursed by Noah and relegated to slavery. She would have liked to think that instead, it was so named by one who looked with pity upon the tragedy of a poverty-stricken people and connected it with the Shakespearean hero who also suffered "the slings and arrows of outrageous fortune."

Jerusalem, that Sunday afternoon, however, was neither pitiable nor unhappy. Instead, as Deborah stared wide-eyed at the foot tapping, backslapping congregation raising to the oaken beams of the ceiling their voices to God, a curious quiver raised little white bumps on her arms. When Delia started shouting, arms waving and doing double time up and down the aisle, Deborah found herself on uncertain steps toddling behind her and joining the chorus of amens and praises.

"Lord, have mercy!" Somebody shouted. "There go Mr. Jacob's daughter."

"God done made them little legs stronger," Ginger shouted.

And their music. Without accompaniment they sang a pot-

16

pourri of melody, now a moaning sadness, now a lilt of hope, and always that unique rhythm that flowed unhampered "in full-throated ease." One day many years hence, when Deborah watched the gray satin-clad figure of Marian Anderson at a concert in the state capital, she would recognize strains of those earlier mellifluous voices emanating from the trained singer's mastery of their deep rich music.

Too soon Ginger was gone. Her big heart found lodging with Rufus, who spirited her away up north. Deborah felt a twinge of jealousy that her friend now could enjoy the miracle of snow and the cold glitter of stars on ice-laden branches.

Long before Ginger's flight north, Deborah was reading. The time came when Deborah had a Bible, proving that she could read even before her legs were steady and sturdy enough to run with other four year olds. How she delighted in deviating from the story of "shepherds abiding in the field by night" and launching into pigs riding camels and newborn lambs butting their older brothers. These digressions would bring giggles from Gamin and stern reprimands from Jacob, which promised a whipping after prayers for laughing at a little sister who was "doing the best she could." Beryl delighted in Deborah's pranks and the subsequent punishment for Gamin, for she knew that her little sister could read far better than Gamin and relished his comeuppance from one so young. Deborah, now the pampered baby, continued to devil Gamin with impunity while the others gloried in the little vixen snaring the fox.

After the readings the family always knelt together as Jacob offered prayers for his family and his neighbors, and he usually invoked the Almighty to strengthen De-Borah's body and send Mount Tabor rain to put food on the table and a few more dollars in the fruit jar buried in the smokehouse under the green pine straw upon which the fresh pork was laid preceding the curing. These silver dollars could buy land cheap in depression years when an acre of cleared land went for a dollar. Like his English forebears, he believed land—not money—meant dignity, class, and respectability. A man who was worth his salt accumulated enough property to settle each of his children off with land upon which to build and plant.

One of the stirring memories of Deborah's childhood was the day Daddy lifted her down from his massive shoulder and placed her unsteady feet on the new ground he had been clearing—his latest purchase of woods bought at forty cents an acre. Gripping her hand firmly in his calloused ones roughened by lathe, grubbing hoe, and axe, he spoke reverently, using the formal address reserved for the most serious discussions. "Daughter, as far as this land goes down, it belongs to us."

Deborah, to whom Santa Claus had brought a globe last Christmas, asked, "Daddy, how far is that? Does it go across as far as China or Africa?"

"Child, what questions you do ask. Sometime I just don't know where you came from. God must have a special mission for you. You might end up a missionary like Sister Laura in India."

"That would suit me fine. I read that in India cows are sacred. I wouldn't ever have to drink another glass of milk. Even with Ovaltine I don't like it much. It's better with coffee, but Mama says I'm too young to drink coffee. Seems like I'm too young for everything. Beryl says if I don't drink milk and get strong, Mama won't ever let me go to school on the bus. Daddy, why won't Mama let me be like other children? I'm fatter than any little girl in Mount Tabor, because Mama makes me wear two undershirts over my tallow plaster on my chest and a sweater and a coat. I just hate Mama sometimes."

His voice was stern like the kind he used with the boys when they were squabbling. "De-Borah, don't you ever say that again. Your mother suffered death to bring you in the world."

"Daddy, I didn't ask to be born. I know how babies get here. I may be little, but I'm smart. And Daddy, my name is Deborah, not De'Borah. It's pretty that way. And Daddy, why won't Mama let me move out of your room at night? Why can't I go to school? I can read better than Cousin Vernie, and she's in the third grade.

I even know my tables to five." Deborah was on a run now.

Jacob stopped her with "I'll study on it." That was the stock reply on matters about which he couldn't decide. His boot toed a root, dislodging it from the black dirt. At that moment Gypsy galloped across the new ground and headed toward the field green with new oats. "I bet a nickel Gamin left the barnyard gates unbarred. Course, that mare could have broken out of her stall again. I just don't know where she came from. I can't tame her to save my soul."

Deborah smiled and thought silently. "She ought to be named Pegasus or—maybe Deborah," she added.

That night when Daddy thought she was asleep and before he humped Mama, he said, "Anna, it's time for Deborah to have her own room. And when school starts in September, I'll tell Mr. Joseph to see her safely on and off the bus." It was not often that Jacob issued an ultimatum. Anna recognized the uselessness of argument.

Deborah squeezed herself tight and rolled over to pleasant dreams, not hearing the frequent moans and grunts that came from Mama and Daddy's bed.

On Christmas, the year before Deborah turned eight, visions of sugarplums did not dance in her head, but the prospect of school bells in September rang in her ears. December was abnormally mild. The frost had not sweetened the collards growing in the vegetable garden, but summer tomatoes still clung to the vines and reddened in winter sun. Even in the deep South, there should have been several freezing nights to accommodate the yearly slaughter of pigs, nightmares for Deborah, who stuffed her fingers in her ears to muffle the sharp ping of the rifle and who turned sick at the sight of scraped white naked bodies dangling from scaffolds on the smokehouse, their slit throats dripping blood into basins. Come December, the radio boomed songs about white Christmas and sleighs, and snowmen. In the Low Country of South Carolina every four or five years a few stray flakes of snow frolicked down to death on warm black earth. Nobody made up songs about Christmas in the South. White paradises belonged to the Yankees, who really didn't deserve them. When they had last visited the South, they not only stole great grandmother's silver thought safe buried under the oak tree but also burned the barn along with the crop of corn and fodder. What saved the house, Daddy said, was the Masonic Emblem on the front door. General Sherman was a Shriner. So somewhere, up north, children were eating snow ice cream with Grandmother's coin silver spoons. It just wasn't fair—hog-killing, hot Christmases and the same old baby toys every year. There would be another baby doll, another tea set painted in garish orange and stamped on the back *Made in China*. Nobody in the world could drink anything from thimble-size cups. And another embroidery kit, a companion to last year's still wrapped in cellophane. There would not even be an innocuous ball to bounce outside on the chimney on a sunny day. No, it wasn't fair, and Deborah had a strict personal code. When she played Jack Stone with Marlene, her imaginary playmate, the name gleaned from one of Beryl's *True Love and Romances* magazine, Deborah didn't cheat a bit when it was Marlene's turn to play and sometimes, though rarely, Marlene won.

The most exciting gift from the mythical rotund, bearded, red-coated annual visitor was a box of sparklers. Bundled and buttoned into her overcoat, despite summer in December, Deborah was allowed to venture as far as the front porch to light her sparklers and watch the others explode their more powerful fireworks in the yard. She had no desire for noisy firecrackers, but sparklers and roman candles transformed flat Mount Tabor into another world where meteors shot across a dark sky and diamonds shimmered and fanned out in her hands. So Deborah waited patiently for September.

Long before Eliot designated April the cruelest month and Pound pronounced anathema on spring, Deborah might have added her own imprecations the year she turned eight. After diphtheria and measles that ran through Mount Tabor paying call to each house, Deborah succumbed to the dreaded pneumonia for the third time. The illness itself was not so bad, despite the hot mustard plasters on her chest to burn out the congestion. It was a time when Deborah was suspended between two worlds. Funny things happened. The pictures of Old Ma and Old Pa (the two ugliest people she had ever seen), which had always hung over the mantel, now could move down and sit temporarily on the shelf by the eight-day clock. Once she saw their stern old faces soften and their lips spread into a smile. One day Dr. Johnson's bald head sprouted red spiky hair that made him look like a fat pixie. In spite of herself she couldn't stop laughing. Mama stood by the bed wringing her hands and wailed, "She's dying, doctor." Did living mean that she'd have to abandon the cute little snowmen that floated around the ceiling, never dropping a flake, and put Old Ma and Old Pa back in their frames with their grimaces permanently frozen on their faces? And the music was nice, too. It was like a song made by raindrops pattering on the tin roof. Deborah couldn't quite decide. If she died, Mama might be sorry that she hadn't let her go to school. Beryl would miss her. Beryl would have no one to tell her secrets—like breaking up with Hubert. Deborah wondered what she and Hubert broke together. She hoped it was that glass marked with ounces from which she drank that hated milk twice a day. Well, they must all be expecting her to die. Hannah, Belle, and Lily, now all safely married, were there. Hannah and Belle were both walking spraddle legged, their stomachs poked out with babies. It was April after all. Maybe they had come for her birthday, but when Gamin and William showed up one night, she decided their presence was not a celebration. Nevertheless, on Easter morning, she heard Dr. Johnson say, "She has passed the crisis." She supposed that meant that she would live. If he had said, "She has passed," and had left it there, it most certainly would have meant a funeral. Sure enough, the music had stopped, the snowmen had disappeared, and Old Ma and Old Pa had again glared at her. Daddy said, "The second miracle is in this room on Easter Sunday. God is telling me some-

21

thing. I can't resist the call any longer." That was the day that Daddy made the vow to preach, a decision that would take him away weekends as he traveled to his country church, Little Shepherd, where he led sinners to the mercy seat, heard their public confessions of sins, and later dunked them in a nearby creek "in the name of the Father, the Son, and the Holy Ghost." Deborah loved Daddy, but she wished he wouldn't preach so loudly and say the same things over and over. Yet he was her strong defender against Mama, who had immediately decided after the bout with pneumonia that school was out. However, Tuesday after Labor Day, without protection of Mama or Daddy, Deborah matriculated into first grade.

CHAPTER

Two

KNEE-DEEP-IN-STOCKINGS

S talwart in courage, Deborah on that warm fall morning, frail under hefty layers of clothes, climbed into the bus, refusing Mr. Joseph's outstretched hand. She headed for a seat next to Cousin Vernie, who was all dressed up in a frilly pink organdy dress with matching socks. Deborah looked down at her skinny legs encased in heavy kneesocks decorated in red, white, and blue triangles. Archie, a tow-headed boy in overalls across the aisle, snickered and said, "Here comes Knee-deep-in-stockings." General laughter floated down the bus. Deborah lifted her head a little higher and thought to herself, "But I can read. I bet they never heard of the word *serendipity*." With that she settled herself beside Vernie.

Their destination was a white-framed schoolhouse sprawled across a half acre of flat ground with an artesian well of water flowing continuously from the rock bed deep in the earth. Gram-

23

mar school housed grades one through seven, and those pupils who finished all courses with passing marks were rewarded with a formal graduation to the newly built brick high school across the road. Along the way and before compulsory school attendance until sixteen, many less apt souls made exits—some to follow behind a plow, some to become early brides and mothers, and some simply to disappear in the faceless flat terrain or in the deep gloom of a wood, with swamp and murky waters. Needless to say, Union Grove populace boasted no darker faces than those having acquired tans during the summer in the cotton and tobacco fields. Little Hamlet, three miles away as the crow flies, was the site of the academy for colored children. From the bus window Deborah had spotted a gaggle of them strolling along barefoot. "Why don't they have a bus, Vernie?"

Vernie shook her head from side to side to acknowledge such an idiot question. "You know," she returned, "we don't ride with them."

"Well, it's not fair," the moron replied.

"Didn't you hear what Miss Effie told us in Sunday school? God put a curse on them and turned them black and made them our slaves."

"Then I don't think God was fair," Deborah returned quickly. "He could have punished them some other way. He could have made them drink fifteen glasses of milk a day without Ovaltine."

Vernie, wide-eyed at such a pronouncement against the Almighty, gasped. "Deborah Jernigan, I'd be afraid God would strike me dead for saying such a thing. Who you think you are to talk against Jesus?"

"It wasn't Jesus who did it. He loved everybody. Besides, Miss Effie was telling a story from the Old Testament. I read another story about why they are black. Apollo, the Greek god of the sun, drove his chariot drawn by powerful horses across the sky every day to bring the sun. One morning his son decided to get up early and drive the team himself. His Daddy kept telling him he was too young. I reckon he was like my brother, Gamin. He never listens and minds nobody. Anyway, Phaeton, I think that was his name, I get him mixed up with Icarus, the boy who flew too close to the sun and his wax wings melted, well, Phaeton lost control of the horses and came too close to the earth and the people's skin turned black. It doesn't say anything about them being slaves. I think that story is more exciting, don't you?"

Vernie couldn't be bothered with such strange stories that her cousin got from books from the traveling library. She wasn't about to have her tagging around behind her. In fact, she wasn't going to let on to anybody that they were kin, with her all diked up in kneesocks and sweater in September. She could just hear everybody laughing at this weirdo. No siree! Deborah Jernigan was on her own. So Vernie turned toward the window to watch the bus heave now into second gear in preparation to pull into Union Grove school yard.

The yellow bus crawled into the circular driveway behind another one already empty of its cargo. The gasping motor dead, Mr. Joseph pulled the lever to open the door. Vernie, along with everyone else, scrambled into the aisle to join the screeching mob. Mr. Joseph's hand motioned them back.

"Hold it. I promised this little girl's Daddy to help her out. She's always been sickly, and this is her first day in school."

So it was that Deborah descended on the arm of Mr. Joseph, who literally lifted her down the last step. With cheeks burning and tears close, Deborah fled the path of the ensuing horde. Mounting the wooden steps alone as fast as she could, she tripped on the seventh step and scraped her knee. Grateful that the others had already passed her, she recovered quickly and pulled the sock a bit higher to absorb the blood. The sleeve of her red sweater brushed the tears now flowing copiously from equally red eyes. "Damn," she whispered. She had said the forbidden word, but she hadn't put the other word behind it. "I asked you, God, to not let me fall. I guess you forgot." Anyway, it was better than having Mama bringing her to school and gripping her hand as she did when they went shopping. So raising herself to her full height, just under four feet, and smoothing her straight bangs cut level above her glistening brown eyes, Deborah, pronounced *DEB*, a stalk on unsteady legs, entered Miss Agatha's first grade class, already filled with thirty odd bodies, and stuffed herself into a back seat. Miss Agatha, the wife of the county magistrate, just missed being rotund. In fact, it was a joke that Magistrate Pope and his spouse not only looked alike but also weighed alike and wielded the stick alike, he the billy on Saturday night to re-calcitrant drunks and she the paddle to the bottoms of erring pupils. Deborah, however, entertained no fear of either of these formidable beings. Magistrate Pope patted her head when he stopped by the family store and always made the same comment: "Growing like a weed, Mr. Jacob." As for Miss Agatha, of whom she had heard but whom she had not met, Deborah planned to be her star pupil and could not imagine being victim to her teacher's wrath. Fortified by her knowledge of the alphabet, the tables, and *Baby Ray*, primer for first grade for twenty years (not to speak of her intimacy with King James and Beryl's copies of *Modern Romance* magazine), Deborah entered the classroom and found an empty desk close to the door.

Miss Agatha's desk stood on a raised platform upon which also rested a speaker's stand. She stood behind the rostrum in front of her charges. She was an imposing figure, but Deborah decided, despite the sternness of her blue piercing gaze and the blond hair skinned back into a tight topknot from which no wisp strayed, that a new scholar was about to make an impression. In her left hand Miss Agatha held a stack of rectangular flashcards. She drew a card from the middle, much like the gypsy in a story in which she had foretold the marriage of a hapless orphan to a prince. Deborah smiled as the word *castle* appeared in bold black letters. Before Miss Agatha could speak, the voice from the back desk sang out, "CASTLE, C-A-S-T-L-E."

Miss Agatha's gold-rimmed glasses slipped slightly down her nose as she perused the hefty little girl in winter apparel and taller than the others. Deborah felt a sudden surge of intellectual pride. She would show them. Knee-deep-in-stockings, indeed. Miss Agatha drew another card.

"Rooster," Deborah crowed. She was about to spell out the word when Miss Agatha stopped her.

"Never mind, Miss Smarty. What is your name?"

"Deborah Marlene Jernigan." Her imaginary playmate sounded so good as a middle name. "Capital D—"

"That's enough Deborah Marlene Jernigan. I can spell. Suppose you give somebody else a chance."

Something is wrong, Deborah thought. Miss Agatha doesn't understand. I was just trying to show her that I could read and maybe I can be put up in the second grade. My sister Hannah made three grades in one year. Of course, there is some mistake. I won't spell the next word.

"KITTEN." This time the voice was softer with just a hint of a plea for understanding. Miss Agatha slapped the cards down on her desk and unhooked a paddle hanging from a nail on the side. As she brandished it in front of the class, Deborah could read clearly the words notched in red letters on the side.

27

CHAPTER

Three

BOARD OF EDUCATION

"Come to the front, Deborah Marlene Jernigan." Years afterward on sleepless nights, Deborah would close her eyes and see that flaming sword, hear three sharp whacks, and feel the burning pain penetrating her heavy layers of clothes. Worst of all was the titter and the smug smiles of the others, suppressing laughter lest they be next to bend over Miss Agatha's ample knee. As she stumbled blindly down the aisle between rows of desks, determined not to add tears to her humiliation, she whimpered inwardly. Rage and hurt collided. "It's not fair. It's not fair." How many times would she think those words, some voiceless, as they were now, some raised in high protest against the injustice around her.

At recess as she waited her turn to drink from the artesian well, she tasted notoriety for the first time. Every Tom, Dick, and Harry; and every Mary, Jane, and Nelly, too, knew that she was the first prey to the paddle. Despite their jeers, Deborah detected just a bit of something else. She hadn't cried and she certainly was smart. Admiration? At the same time, she drew a line of demarcation that she could not imagine ever crossing. Strangely enough, the news of her disgrace never reached Mama and Daddy, and Deborah hugged it close to her, not sharing it even with Beryl, who would have taken on Miss Agatha in defense of her little sister. Instead, the memory cut a swathe into her heart. Her teacher must have later realized her mistake because she never again raised her voice to her brightest pupil, who might also have skipped three grades except for a new law against advancing pupils that rapidly. But Deborah never forgave her. Miss Agatha remained the wicked witch of fairyland and the villain who stalked the helpless and unwary innocents. At Christmas Miss Agatha gave all the girls except Deborah in first grade a little box of ceramic dolls donated by the local dime store. On Deborah's desk appeared a second-hand copy of *David Copperfield*. Deborah never said, "Thank you."

To an eight year old, taller by a foot than her classmates, five grades ahead of them in achievement, and nil in playground performance, first grade was not the utopia about which Deborah had dreamed. She learned nothing about the three R's except to develop a fancy unreadable cursive, which she imagined to be appropriate for her isolated state. Her front teeth now began to protrude, a feature complementing the oddity of her dress and stature. She walked with a slump, ate her lunch alone at recess, and looked down her nose behind her round gold-framed eyeglasses. Mama's optometrist had discovered a weak left eye just like Mama's. Ugly duckling and genius, and labeled by her peers, Deborah built herself a fortress with a deep moat surrounding it, though no one had the slightest interest in bridging the gulf nor kneeling at her iron door. In her domicile she was happy. She role-played the characters in the books she read and frequently transformed herself into a beautiful girl with curly locks, porcelain skin, and even pearly teeth. Her stylish clothes matched the manikins in Sears Roebuck and Spiegel catalogs. On the days that she had the slightest sniffle, Mama kept her home. Deborah didn't mind. In fact, she sometimes manufactured hoarseness, a guarantee that she could stay in bed and read. The A's that she brought home monthly were no source of pride. They represented no challenge, but a level of excellence for first graders. Gamin, now in high school, was not a good student but made up for his academic deficiency in basketball, a game which he played secretly because Daddy, now a minister, preached against exposing the body in shorts, the attire for athletes, and the betting that went on at games. Consequently, the star of the hardwood was also frequently kept at home when his parents suspected a competition between the local schools.

One day, the principal of the high school paid Deborah a visit. When he came into the class, he whispered something to Miss Agatha. To Deborah's surprise, the tall bald man, suited in coat and tie, was standing by her desk.

"Good morning, Deborah. I hear you are the best student in first grade." Brown eyes scrutinized him and decided it was time for a bit of play.

"Oh, no, sir! You heard it wrong. You see I got a paddling the first day of school. Good students don't get whippings, do they?" Out of the corner of her eye she could see Miss Agatha's face turn beet red. Mr. White, caught quite off guard, stuttered.

"Deborah, I meant your grades."

"Oh, that." Deborah shrugged her shoulders and opened up *Epson's Basic Reader: Fourth Year*, to "Ali Baba and the Forty Thieves."

"Deborah, where is your brother, Gamin? We have a game with Good Hope this afternoon, and he is our best guard."

"Oh, so you didn't come to congratulate me on my grades." Deborah looked up at him and gave him a broad bucktooth smile. "Gamin? Oh, he's at home today helping with the hog-killing," she replied nonchalantly.

"Deborah, do you think that if I went to your house that

your Daddy would let him come to the school for the game?"

"Why, Mr. White, don't you know that playing ball is a sin? Jesus didn't play ball, didn't wear shorts, or bet on games. Remember he drove the moneychangers out of the temple? You wouldn't want Gamin to go straight to hell, would you?" she asked innocently.

"Who told you that tommyrot?"

Deborah's eyes flashed mischievously. In truth, she had no time for all that sinning talk, but now was the time to show Miss Agatha and her classmates that Knee-deep-in-stockings had a tongue unafraid to frustrate this figure of authority.

"Don't you call my Daddy tommyrot," she snapped indignantly. "He reads the Bible every night and preaches against the sins of the flesh every Sunday."

It was now Mr. White's turn to blush. He could not quite decide whether this precocious child was speaking her convictions or was just pulling his leg. He wanted to laugh, but at the same time he had a strong urge to smack her impertinence. Instead, he reiterated, "Do you think Daddy would let Gamin come play this afternoon if I begged him?"

"Beg all you please. You have about as much chance in getting him to play as I have getting promoted to the fourth grade at the end of the year." With that she opened her fourth grade reader and continued putting the thieves in the jars supposedly filled with oil.

All eyes were on her now. Gosh, that Knee-deep-in-stockings had a nerve. Imagine talking back to a principal who had an electric paddle that he used when he got tired of whipping. What would this great man do?

This great man walked slowly out the door. That afternoon Union Grove lost to Good Hope, and Gamin Jernigan quit school to work on the farm and help out in the family grocery store. His pockets were always full from the till, and boxes of chocolate-covered cherries mysteriously disappeared to a number of young ladies. At the end of the year Deborah was promoted to fourth grade. Daddy said it was another miracle. It was right there in the Bible. Another Jacob had struggled with the angel and followed the commandment to preach. And just look what happened. His child had received a blessing. Deborah smiled to herself. She knew where the credit belonged—to a bald-headed man who recognized that a mere first grader—and a girl to boot—had got his goat. What Deborah didn't know was that Harold White, though he had lost his best basketball player, thought Union Grove might be able to score in county literary competitions. This little upstart had actually won the spelling bee for grammar school. Besides, he enjoyed amusing his friends with the encounter and played the hero at the end of the story by bending state rules allowing her to skip aging Miss Minnie's second and frivolous Fanny's third. Cousin Vernie, who at last got promoted to fourth, was not pleased. To save face, she spread it around that the teachers felt sorry for Deborah being so sickly and thought she would be dead before finishing grammar school. Deborah sometimes thought about the possibility, but she did not worry about it particularly, feeling a certain pride that Hannah could no longer brag so much about skipping grades. A little battle weary, she eased through fourth grade without open confrontation with teacher or classmate.

CHAPTER

Four

SANTA'S DEMISE

It was Christmas Eve again and one of those days which felt like the first of May and barefoot time; yet the brown grass, bare oak trees, and dried stalks of summer marigolds defied spring. Deborah sat on the cement steps and wondered what a white Christmas would be like. Here, it was warm sunshine. There was not even a light freeze to send you snuggling in a feather bed under mounds of quilts. What was the word she had spelled that had won her the spelling bee? *Anachronism.* She smiled remembering the startled looks when she, a mere first grader, had spelled down a seventh grader. Why she hadn't even known what it meant. Curiosity had sent her to the dictionary. Anachronism was like the weather, spring in winter. All day long the radio had been playing Yankee songs: "I'm Dreaming of a White Christmas," and "A Winter Wonderland." The book she had been reading had told such lovely stories of ice hanging like

33

glass beads from hawthorn and birch and snowmen with pipes and red hats and drifting snowflakes with each snowflake different. Once it had snowed in Mount Tabor for two whole hours. She had stood with her nose mashed to the windowpane, trying to feel its coldness. Of course, Mama wouldn't let her go out for fear of her catching cold and sore throat. Then the sun had come and turned the feathered whiteness to black slush. Frankly, she was tired of sun. She didn't feel sunny inside. There had been a dark heaviness under her heart so long that she felt it belonged to her. Maybe she was having a heart attack and would prove Vernie's point.

A solitary ant ambled across the steps after the crumbs she had dropped from Mama's black fruitcake sample. Had he lost his friends? There had been a cold snap last week. Ants were supposed to be smart creatures. Surely he hadn't been dumb enough to be left behind. She had never liked crawly things. But this little fellow was different. Maybe he was an anachronism, too. How lucky he was that she had dropped the crumb! How lucky would she be tonight? She idly pondered the difference between luck and God. Were they the same? Anyway, she was willing to believe in both of them if it would do any good. Santa Claus was coming. She would go to bed early as she had the last seven Christmases that she could remember. She would say her prayers like a good little Christian and throw in a few to lady luck for good measure. She probably wouldn't go to sleep and relive other years when she had heard Mama and Daddy put her toys near the warm hearth in their bedroom. The sounds had told her what she was getting. Her ears had followed the tightening of each screw on the red wagon and the clatter of the china tea set as Mama put the cups in the saucers to display them on the miniature tea table. Always there was the queer sound, neither animal nor human, coming from the baby doll as Daddy turned her over to see if she could cry. Why did they think that she still believed that there was a Santa Claus coming down the chimney all over the whole wide world, bringing all children what they wanted if they had been good? Once she had ventured to ask Daddy if Santa was for real. He had patted her benevolently on the knee and said that there would always be a Santa Claus as long as she believed in him. Santa was the Spirit of Christmas and never forgot good little girls. She wondered what Daddy would say if he could look inside of her. It seemed too much trouble to argue the point, and Daddy was so pleased with his explanation. If she didn't make such good grades in school, she would wonder if Daddy didn't think her "teched in the head" like Aunt Rosa's Timothy. That part about "spirit" had interested her. She had no faith in sleighs and reindeer, but there might be something a way out there that could influence Mama and Daddy. Not the God in Sunday school, for he got mad with people and sent them to that horrible place that good little girls never dared utter—a place where it never snowed not even for two hours. Well, you had to believe in something, and since she and God had not been on such good terms since he had let her down on that first day of school, she might just as well believe in the Spirit of Christmas. To the Spirit of Christmas she would pray tonight for a bicycle. But if it couldn't manage that, please let her not get another baby doll. Everybody in the fifth grade would find out.

She had already helped the Spirit of Christmas out. The letter to Santa Claus was in the bottom of the trash can so Mama and Daddy knew. What a moron they must think her! Ten years old and still believing in a little fat man who, when he laughed, shook "like a bowl full of jelly." Where would they hide the bicycle? She hadn't snooped. She might not find it. It would be too big for the house or the trunk of Daddy's car. Of course, there was the store or the barn. Her eyes perused the gray clapboard hulk across the road. It looked a little like the sick hen before she died, what with its drooping sheds on each side of the hayloft. That would be a likely spot except somebody had stolen bushels of corn a few weeks ago. Smokehouses were out, too. Even now she could smell the hickory wood curing the fresh hams and shoulders from the last hog killing. She hated those mornings when she couldn't help hearing the ping of the rifle, one for each pig. Gamin called her a sissy. She supposed all older brothers were like him. He was the one who had finished her completely with dolls. It had been her first baby doll with hair, Mabelline, because her painted eyebrows were arched like the picture on the make-up advertisement. Her coarse reddish brown hair, parted from the stick center of her head, fell to her shoulders in Shirley Temple curls. Although the hair looked remarkably like the wig Aunt Fanny wore after she had typhoid fever, at least it was curly, not straight like her own. Mabelline wore a rather pretty dress, pink organdy spattered with tiny white daises that touched just the top of her ribbed white socks above her white slippers. Mabelline was a movie star. She had been all over the world, singing and dancing and having fun, and had never been lonely, for she had friends—dozens of them in every city in the world. Deborah wasn't lonely with her either. She would set her on the dresser surrounded by cutouts from Sears Roebuck catalog and pictures from magazines from faraway exciting places. Gamin had died laughing. "Dead doll and dead people. I'm sure glad I wasn't born a dumb girl." It was true. The china blue eyes fringed with the thick stubble of brown hair and her painted waxen face stared ahead the way that she had imagined great grandmother was looking behind her closed eyelids when she lay in the long gray box with silver tassels in the front parlor. It was true. She was dumb. Gamin was right.

Gamin was backing the car out of the driveway. She would pretend that she wouldn't see him. "Deb, dreaming about Santa Claus," he yelled as he roared out of the driveway the way he always did when Daddy wasn't home.

That was it. The bicycle was at Aunt Fanny's house. Gamin would bring it home when he came in from his date. She just knew it. Her heart gave a wild leap that sent her blood surging into the heavy spot. She would have faith like what Daddy said. "Faith will move mountains," though she couldn't quite see why anyone would want to move a mountain. Faith was to believe just as hard as you could and push out the dark shadows which lay in the middle of the heavy spot beneath her pounding heart. She wouldn't snitch on her faith this time. Perhaps that was what happened to her in first grade. Her faith had not even been the size of a mustard seed. She would make herself go to sleep tonight. But if she couldn't, she would press her ears tight when Gamin came in. She wouldn't hear him take the bike, her bike, from the top of the car, tied with a rope to keep it secure. Tomorrow morning in her stocking hanging over the fireplace, there would be a note written in red letters. LOOK ON THE PORCH. She would run to Mama and Daddy and hug them harder than she could remember. Then she would fly to the porch. She would call it *Meteor* and learn to ride it right away. By afternoon she might ride it by Vernie's house, not to stop but just to let her see it. That's the way it would be. It wouldn't rain either or turn cold so Mama wouldn't worry about her catching a sore throat. It just took a little faith in the Spirit of Christmas when everybody was supposed to be happy.

It was just the way she had planned. She drank her milk without complaint and volunteered to go to bed early so that she could get up early for Santa Claus. Mama felt her forehead to see if she had a fever. Daddy nodded knowingly that their little girl still believed in Santa Claus. She didn't even cringe at Mama's goodnight kiss and the usual "my baby" which she had been saying every night since Deborah moved into her own room.

Once the lights were out, she pressed her hands hard over her eyes. The bright colors whirled around changing shapes until they formed a red bicycle with *Meteor* painted in shooting white stars on the side. She didn't even hear Gamin come in. Somehow, she had managed to throw herself in the white spirit of Christmas and fall into the land of real sleigh bells and swirls of snowflakes and snowmen riding red bicycles on top of icy glass mountains.

The next morning she was awakened by a suspicious sound like the drizzle of rain. It couldn't rain on the day she got her bicycle. It was a bad sign. But by afternoon it might clear up and she had to keep believing right up to the last minute. She would count to one thousand by fives, very slowly. Then she would go to see. Five—ten—fifteen—twenty...

There was a globe of the earth and a pencil box and a green sweater with white reindeer prancing across the front, and a pair of red galoshes and a blue tam with a cottony bow on the top and an embroidery set and water colors and two boxes of chocolate-covered cherries and five boxes of sparklers. Not even a stocking this year to hide a note. In the middle of it all, arranged like a display in a toyshop, sat a princess doll.

"Deborah." Mama's voice was coming from the bed. "Don't you like the doll? Santa Claus brought her, but I made the dress. It's just like Mama's wedding dress. I found the same kind of lace to make the yoke. Santa didn't think you are old enough for a bike. You could fall and break an arm or leg. Maybe next year. Mama wanted her baby to have the prettiest doll around. She has a key that fits into her back. I left an opening in the dress and petticoat. You can wind her up and she can say 'Mama.'"

The embers of last night's fire were dying in the fireplace. Deborah's eyes focused on red coals thinly coated with ash. What they needed was a little help to bolster flames. Deborah seized the princess doll and flung her into their midst. Black ribbons ran up her voluminous net skirt as the waxen face melted into some grotesque stillborn fetus. Mama, moving faster than Deborah had ever seen her, grabbed the poker and dragged the corpse from the inferno. For a moment Deborah thought that she would strike her. Instead, Mama sobbed brokenly. "Baby, how could you do this to me?"

"Mama, don't ever call me baby again."

Still in her woolen nightgown, Deborah rushed headlong out the door into December rain that mixed with her tears. As she stumbled over a root of the live oak tree, Daddy's hand steadied her.

"It's all right De'Borah. Don't cry. You're a big girl now."

"It's not fair, Daddy," she whispered. "It's not fair." His

big arm encircled her waist, and although he said nothing, she sensed his understanding that lightened just a little the heaviness around her heart.

CHAPTER

Five

THE BUTTON

With trembling fingers Deborah pushed the long rows of buttons into their loops on the back of Beryl's navy wedding dress. The top button just below the hairline lost its anchorage and rolled across the pine floors and under the dresser. In the absence of electric lights, procuring the tiny globule necessitated a witch-hunt with Deborah scrambling on her all-fours while she pawed frantically to retrieve it.

"I'm so sorry. I'll find it. Don't be mad." These whispered regrets were meant to keep them from Mama, who now would be fleeing the house through the back door to take refuge in the woods where she could share her grief with wind, tree, and bird over the loss of her fourth daughter. That pattern of behavior had its inception when Belle eloped, was repeated with each marriage, and therefore was as much a part of the ceremony of marriage in the Jernigan household as "I do" or "I will." Anna Jernigan

40

vociferously opposed sharing one of her children with either sex and registered her protest with an abrupt exodus accompanied by woeful wails. On the scene, however, was Jacob Jernigan, who waited patiently in the parlor for the nervous prospective in-law to ask for her hand in marriage or to give a son last minute admonitions. Later, when the couple would have escaped in a vehicle—never marked with "Just Married"—Jacob would comfort his wife with his "Tut Tut's" and perhaps remind her with a "Well, Anna, remember we got married. It's part of God's plan."

Deborah on the floor had relived the whole scenario but felt it a good omen that she had actually found the lost button, although there was little hope of making reparations as she heard Robert's Chevrolet door slam. She surveyed her sister—playmate, mother, and teacher—and felt tears, which she would refuse to shed, sparkle in her brown eyes behind her round gold-framed spectacles.

"How do I look, Deborah? Never mind the button. It won't show. Oh, Deb! I'm so scared."

"Don't be," Deborah soothed. The stories she had read all told of the magic of the wedding night so she wondered why her big sister should be so afraid. And she was so beautiful! Her dark brown hair was drawn from a high forehead and clustered at the nape of her neck in three tiered double rows. Over each ear a single curl dropped, adding a classic touch to what would otherwise have been a spartan hair-do. Jernigan girls did not cut their hair. A woman's hair was her glory, according to the Apostle Paul and, therefore, her locks should go unshorn. Amazing, Deborah mused, how the Bible dictated almost every aspect of life—enforced by the rod "which spared not the child," and the church, that governing body that issued its stern edicts prohibiting a Saturday night movie or indulging, except for medicinal purposes, in anything stronger than black coffee. Beryl's white cheeks bore only the faintest hint of color lest she follow the infamous Jezebel, whose fate every Sunday school scholar knew. In those meanderings Deborah envied her big sister, who, once she closed the

Jernigan door behind her, could make her own rules that might permit bobbed hair and eye shadow as well as wearing shorts in summer to show off shapely legs. Life inside the Jernigan portals held little glamour or romance except for the radio and books, two avenues of escape. Of course, there were daydreams, spun out of "airy nothingness," invisible in the darkness of a room at midnight or in the mid-morning light of a Sunday sermon, where the preacher pontificated on the sins of the flesh and the power that could transform scarlet into snow white.

"Beryl, why isn't your dress white? Aren't you a virgin? Brides shouldn't be wearing navy. That's for grass widows. How come you chose navy?"

Deborah knew the answer. The question was designed to add levity to temper the charged atmosphere. The dress had been surreptitiously acquired from the pages of the couturier Sears Roebuck which featured no pristine gowns that season. It had been carefully secreted within the folds of Beryl's brown winter coat away from the watchful eyes of Mama, who could smell a conspiracy even before it was hatched.

Beryl's reply accompanied the pinch that she so frequently bestowed upon her sibling. It descended usually in the neighborhood of the upper arm but on rare occasions such as this one, landed on Deborah's nose. It was a gentle playful tweak that acknowledged both the wickedness of the smart-mouth interrogation and the affection that had prompted it.

"What do you know about virgins and wedding dresses? All you know is what you read in books. When you get married, if Mama lets you out of her sight long enough, you'll be in black— old enough to have grandchildren."

"I bet I know about as much as you do about sex. Remember when you and I built a coop to force an old hen to set when she hadn't had the company of a cock-a-doodle-do? Those biddies that were going to be ours turned into twelve smashed eggs and a peach tree switch on your bottom. Course, I was too young to know better. But a teenager! How dumb can you be?"

"Dumb enough to let you pull a button off my dress." Her long, slender fingers tucked the open loop under her high-necked dress, which fell in flared softness over her hips and down below her knees. On the bed lay the cardboard suitcase, a dun brown on the outside, but which housed the baby blue gown and negligee, her wedding night apparel. Deborah had touched its softness and transformed its rayon satin into gossamer wisps of lace and silk.

"Mr. Jacob, I come to ask you for Beryl. We are going to get married. We want your blessing." Robert's words were delivered in a voice loud enough for both of them to hear, but they came out staccato notes disjointed and disconnected. At the same time Beryl lifted the suitcase from the bed and surveyed the room where she had slept both child and woman and now soon to be wife. Last night she had slept in uninterrupted slumber. The anodyne for anxiety had been a double dose of Mama's red nervine, potent enough to prolong sleep through breakfast, which Mama so rarely prepared. Now she looked at her airless hermitage, its walls lined with hooks upon which her dresses still hung. The mirror caught the reflection of two sisters, one a skinny child with bangs cut straight across large brown eyes now spilling with tears; the other, a young woman, her heart beating wildly, as she strained to hear her father's reply.

"Robert, if you can't take care of her, you know where you got her." It was a simple statement, not meant to intimidate nor offend. It was a father's assertion that whatever the circumstances, this child of his loins would always find a home under his lintel. At the same time there was a note of sadness as he once again transferred the well-being of a daughter into the hand of a stranger. Unlike the Jacob of old, who had had many sons and one daughter, whose wedding night ended in bloody tragedy, Jacob Jernigan had had more daughters than sons. Perhaps the pious Jacob remembered the fabled Diana and prayed the nuptial feast of his daughter would be joyous. Like the Jacob of old, he had wrestled with many angels, not the least among them his wife, Anna. What had become of the dark-haired beauty he had courted and won? Somewhere in the subterranean recesses of a disturbed mind, this Low Country belle had receded into the whining termagant of *Ethan Frome* ilk. Now that Beryl was gone, there would only be Deborah, who would listen to the break in his voice at morning prayers around the kitchen table as he asked his God to give him strength and perseverance.

"Mr. Jacob, I intend to take care of her." The sentence was spoken as prayerfully as a vow uttered in front of an altar alight with myriad candles. This tall young man, without land or prospects as Anna had reminded Beryl many times, stood stalwart before his father-in-law, perhaps avowing that one day he would be counted with no less love and trust as Jacob's elder son.

Beryl picked up the suitcase. "You forgot the button," Deborah whispered. It sat in the palm of her small hand like an amulet, the color of lapis lazuli, the semi-precious stone found in prehistoric caves decorating the tombs of ancient man, the stone in mosaics adorning the walls of medieval cathedrals. Blue would always be, as it was for the Blessed Mother, Mary, Beryl's favorite color.

Beryl's hand closed Deborah's fingers around the button. "You keep it. It will be our secret. On your wedding day I'll sew it on the front of your white dress." With a final pinch, this time on her sister's neck just above her heart, Beryl moved toward the front door.

The old Chevy gave a disheartened heave and then caught new life as it settled into the dark ruts of the dirt country road that led to the newly paved highway. Deborah neither saw nor heard the departure. Like her mother she had fled to share her grief and joy with wood, wind, and sky.

CHAPTER

Six

HANNAH

W hen Deborah was eleven, the dark angel swooped down over Hannah's house. In prior months Deborah had drawn closer to her sister. Beryl had always been her favorite, but now that she had married and moved away, Deborah sometimes drifted over to Hannah's house at the Jess Place, so-called because of its former owner. Daddy had bought the farm at a good price and had given it to Hannah as a wedding present. Motherhood had mellowed Hannah, though her intellectual superiority still remained evident. Strangely enough, the man she had chosen to marry was no brain, and Deborah suspected that the impetus to find a husband was due to the fact that her younger sister, Belle, had preceded her in matrimony. Hannah, like Deborah, loved books. Everybody recognized Hannah's proficiency in Holy Scripture. Not even Daddy was a match for her. She taught the adults in Sunday school class, which Deborah elected to attend. Many of Hannah's pupils claimed that she talked a lot more about what was not in the Bible. That "lot" was what fascinated Deborah, who sat entranced as Hannah expounded upon, not just Pharaoh, but the pyramids, Cheops, and the famous library in Alexandria, now forever lost to the world. The mother of two children as well as a meticulous housekeeper, Hannah made time in her busy day to flesh out some dimensional meaning in scripture based upon its cultural, social, and geographic background. She was a devout Baptist but often voiced her disagreement with her church's insistence on male ministry, and though everyone accepted her faith as basically fundamental, she might have been regarded by the more enlightened as an early feminist. Knowing that her gray matter was far weightier than that of her kind, unambitious husband, perhaps she regretted her early marriage that terminated high school in her senior year. At any rate, what she had missed, her children would have. She became a stern monitor of Johnny's homework each night. Unlike Deborah's easiness in goofing off from school, Johnny's ruses never worked. When he said he was too sick to go to school, Hannah put an active little boy to bed and pinned the sheets around his chin, a remedy that sent a healthy lad gladly boarding the bus the next day. Little Emily, who was Hannah's dream child, glued her bright eyes to the page while her mother opened up the world of Joseph of the coat of many colors, who was tossed in the pit by wicked brothers, or the baby Jesus illumined by the star that shone over a humble stable.

One night as Hannah was introducing Johnny to long division, little Emily found the bottle of laxative pills coated with sugar. Intelligent though she was, she could neither read the word *strychnine* on the bottle nor guess that the sweet-tasting caplets were lethal. She ate them all. Hers was the first death Deborah witnessed. It was not the peaceful one described by Daddy as belonging to those who "lived and died with the Lord," but one of horrible gasping, regurgitations, and seizures that shook the small frame.

Two days later Emily's body would lie in a small grave in the churchyard. Hannah, who had barred her doors admitting neither family nor friends, would not see her child's casket lowered into the dark earth. Instead, she remained at home where she occupied herself with a housewife's chores—strange behavior for a grieving mother according to Mount Tabor. Deborah, by choice, remained with her sister but stayed on the front porch occupied with thoughts "too deep for tears," intermittently whispering, "It's not fair." Death had brought her even closer to Hannah, who she suspected was mouthing the same protests. She could hear her sister's movements in the kitchen but dared not join her lest she cry and start Hannah sobbing, who had not shed a tear. So Deborah sat in the rocking chair where she, too, had read to Emily and was grateful not to be a witness to what was happening inside.

There was rightness about Hannah's kitchen. The pots and pans marched in procession flanking the iron stove, replete with warming ovens and reservoirs filled with hot water. The wood box was stacked with hickory and oak, split and cut to stove size. Fruit jars neatly labeled—figs, watermelon preserve, pickled peaches, apple jelly—lined shelves along the wall. Even the blue-checked design of the Priscilla curtains seemed appropriate, for Hannah wore a matching apron tied in a balanced bow over her gray silk Sunday dress. She stood at the heavy oak table which centered the room. Hannah was making biscuits. Before her in the wooden oblong bread tray lay an inert mass of white dough.

Everyone knew that Hannah was the mistress of the bread tray as she was of her husband, John, and their two children. As deftly as she could turn the formless mass of dough into uniform biscuits, bearing the imprint of her fingers, she had managed the household with the precision and good sense required of every farm wife if her family was "to get ahead." Today, however, she stood, her floury hands poised mid-air as though they had lost their way. It was not like her to be inactive. Every waking moment since, as a bride, she had crossed the threshold into this four-room frame house, had been occupied. At the end of the day she still found time to read the scripture or some commentary that clarified and enriched the meaning. In her dreams she moved from the world of books to a bit of her rose garden under the kitchen window to the smocked design she was putting on Emily's Easter dress. If idleness was the devil's workshop, then Hannah was close to Eden. Now she absently moved one hand to right the silver comb in her dark braids which tiered her small head and stared at the window as though she were searching out an intruder standing in her well-kept rose garden. Just day before yesterday she had picked four perfect buds. She remembered suddenly that as her shears had snipped them, a thorn had pricked her finger, drawing a single drop of blood. How stupid of her to be so careless! She had always known how to avoid thorns even without gloves. Now she rubbed the spot on her left index finger which gave no twinge of pain. But the roses had flopped. There they stood in the fruit jar on the windowsill, their heads limp and lifeless. Hannah had forgotten to water them.

"Hannah, it's time to go." It was John standing in his dark blue serge suit speaking in his Sunday voice when he was called on to say a prayer at the close of the service.

Instantly Hannah's hands found their way to the bread tray. With her left hand she squeezed the dough into a tight ball, rounded it in her cupped hands, flattened it with her palms, and placed it in the oven pan, giving it a final pat with two fingers. One after the other she formed neat biscuits, not indicating even with a nod John's presence.

"Hannah, it's time to go," he repeated. "It's hard for me, too." His voice was low and ragged.

"I'm not going, John. I'm going to stay right here and bake these biscuits. You'll need something to eat when you get back."

"Hannah, you can't do this. It's not right. Besides, what will people say? A woman who won't go to her own child's funeral."

Her cupped hands shaped the last piece of dough, and with a quick flip she dropped it into the pan, flattening it so that it was broader and thinner than its companions. She moved to the stove, opened the oven door, and shoved in the pan.

She faced her husband. "I don't care what people think or say. I won't be stared at today. I won't listen to Preacher Thomas or Daddy say that God knows best. I won't listen to such lies. How in the name of common sense could God let what happened to Emily. Only three years old. I'm not listening to that rubbish today."

"Why, Hannah, that's blasphemy. You can't question God. Besides, it was an accident. You mustn't blame yourself and you certainly mustn't blame God."

"So you've said it at last. That's what you and everybody else have been thinking. You've all just been trying to spare my feelings. It was my fault. My negligence. If I hadn't been helping Johnny with his lessons, Emily wouldn't have eaten the candy-coated laxative pills. Well, I can't be in ten places at one time. But God can. He is ubiquitous. Preacher Thomas says so though he's too dumb to know the word." She laughed a brittle laugh as though something were about to break. "If God is everywhere, then where was he? I ask you. Where was he? She thought she was eating candy." Her voice broke, but there were no sobs, not even a tear.

She heard the back screen door close softly. John wouldn't lock the door. They seldom did, not even at night. They had always felt so safe. Who would be out on a country dirt road at night twelve miles from the nearest doctor and fifty miles from a hospital? If only Elsie Parson hadn't decided to have her baby, at least Dr. Baker would have been available to come to little Emily.

She mustn't think. Somehow she must find a way to stop remembering. She had always found ways. She could scarcely remember labor pains. And Daddy's accident with the chain saw was now just a bad dream. What she needed was rest. Pulling the rocker from the corner toward the stove, she felt suddenly cold like when she went out to the potato bank in December to bring up yams for a Christmas pudding. She would rest, and then she would finish dinner. She dropped down into the chair and with hands clenched into tight balls; she stared through the glass door at the biscuits, just beginning to rise. Closing her eyes, she eased her head back against the blue-checked pillow attached to the rocker.

Deborah stood in the doorway. Glad that Hannah was sleeping, she slipped out of the room into her chair on the porch. Her eyes moved across the field to the road now filled with cars and trucks moving slowly toward the church. All that talk about little Emily being called by God to be a rose in his garden sounded like a bad story by someone who couldn't write. In truth in minutes now Emily would be in the grave. She knew exactly why Hannah wouldn't go to the funeral and was grateful that she had been excused to stay with her sister.

Hannah woke with a start. "Oh, my! The biscuits. I'm just in time. John likes them crisp but not burned."

Grabbing a potholder from a rack, she drew them out and for a moment admired her art as she smelled their warm bread goodness. Two years ago at the county fair her biscuits had won first place. Everybody said she ought to enter her recipe in the *Progressive Farmer*. But she could never be definite about the proportions. Her hands seemed to know without head orders. She reached for the wicker breadbasket and began gingerly arranging the biscuits in pyramid fashion. Before putting them into the warmer, she tucked them in a kitchen towel as tenderly as she would cover a baby.

She opened the iron Dutch oven on the top of the stove. The steam momentarily obscured the round roast surrounded by miniature carrots and potatoes in brown gravy. It was ready. But the table had to be set. The room needed tidying.

She decided to use her wedding china, Havilland in pink apple blossom. She was proud of the four-piece setting, just enough for her family. And the lace tablecloth. Why not? It was after all Emily's birthday. Ten years it had taken Aunt Hannah to complete it for her namesake. One day it would be Emily's. John would forgive her for not going to church when he saw how much trouble she had gone to make the table festive. Funny though, she couldn't remember whether Emily was two or three. Oh, well, the dates were all there in the family Bible. Their marriage and the births.

It was ready now. How pretty the table looked. Hannah had found one pink rose in the garden, just right for the centerpiece. How tall it stood in the crystal bud vase! She drew up three oak chairs to the table. Just as she heard John's car in the driveway, she moved Emily's highchair in place, not forgetting to put her bib on the apron.

The screen door opened and closed softly. From the kitchen Hannah called out, "John, would you mind helping Emily change her dress? I don't want her to soil it before Christmas."

Deborah stood in the doorway. She and John looked at each other wordlessly. Hannah, her back turned to them, was busy dishing up the roast. This time Deborah rushed out the door. She did not cry until she had reached the road. In the privacy of her room she poured out the horror that she had witnessed to Marlene.

CHAPTER

Seven

THE DEATH OF MARLENE

Marlene, through grammar school, continued to be Deborah's intimate. She was pretty good at jackstone playing, but Deborah won four times out of five and felt a little sorry for her, actually letting her win on the fifth round. It wasn't that Marlene wasn't a worthy opponent; it was just that Deborah was better. Nevertheless, Deborah was jealous of her invisible playmate's beauty. Marlene was tall and carried herself in queenly fashion—a head luxuriant with Hedy Lamarr curls. Deborah had seen the actress on the cover of loose-leaf notebook paper. Among the multiple commandments, outnumbering by far Moses' ten, were "Thou shalt not go to movies" and "Thou shalt not use makeup." Look what happened to Jezebel of the painted face in scripture. She was thrown to the dogs. Marlene's face was exquisitely made up from sculptured eyebrows to wide blue eyes shadowed by long fringed lashes. Her scarlet lips accented a porcelain face that blushed with color over prominent cheekbones. The chin, always held at a jaunty angle, crowned the long throat, a veritable Nefertiti, whom Deborah had met through *Compton's Encyclopedia*. Here was someone whom Gamin could not kill, a better companion than a doll stuffed with cotton, the epitome, the apotheosis of glamour who could sin with impunity. Deborah, on many occasions—like in the midst of Miss Janie's strident singsong voice jerking out "Paul Revere's Ride" or Poe's "The Raven"—escaped as she whispered smart-ass quips to Marlene, who was also a good listener. Useful as she was as a confidante who never divulged secret, forbidden longings, she served best as the heroine of stories that Deborah spun on long summer evenings when the heavy iron Home Comfort stove, fueled by wood and never completely cooled, intensified the sultry heat in her airless room tucked between the boys' room and the screened in back porch. Lying on a feather mattress, frequently sunned on the hedges framing the walkway to the road, Deborah moved Marlene to snow-capped Alps or cool breezes drifting off Loch Lomond. There she met secretly a blond Lothario with a hint of cruelty in the set of his mocking smile—one who would bring passion and pain but who would eventually succumb to the proud, but long-suffering beauty. The stories had many variations of setting and plot—but always there was the tender reconciliation and the promise of fulfillment. The love scenes and surrender were cast in a dream-like aura similar to an impressionist painting slightly out of focus. Years later in a university library as the spinner of dreams leafed through Dante's *Inferno* or Burton's *Anatomy of Melancholy*, Marlene might be momentarily resurrected and then like the roll of a film fade into a half-recumbent figure poring over the dusty tomes. Often the harsh glare of the single light would soften as illusion eclipsed reality and once more, Deborah, now the heroine, stood wreathed in clouds high above the dust at her feet. In short the dreamer did not die and her tales lay waiting to find a permanent resting place on paper. That would be a long night's journey into day.

Access to the world beyond Mount Tabor had come in a mahogany box with a cathedral dome and strips of woven cloth sliced with wood over its face. The Jernigans were the first in Mount Tabor to get a radio. For once Gamin and William worked peacefully together erecting the pole that was the aerial that would bring the *Grand Old Opry*, *Lum and Abner*, *Baby Snooks*, and *Amos and Andy*. Saturday morning *Let's Pretend* brought audio fairy tales, ultimate reality. Better than fancy was *The Lux Radio Theater*, which introduced Deborah to the world of great drama. One day, above the static that so frequently drowned a broadcast, Deborah's finger tuned in a strange kind of music, different from Roy Acuff and Ernest Tubb. It sounded like the trill of a bird accompanied by strange instruments, not piano, organ, guitar, nor fiddle. Intent on picking up the baseball game, Gamin switched the dial. "Gam," she said, "I heard Daddy say Sarah Rogers was coming to the store with her mama to try on one of the new hats that came in yesterday. I think I hear their pickup," she finished, looking out the window. The Brooklyn Dodgers erased, Deborah's ears reverberated as Lily Pons attenuated high C's in the Bell Song. That afternoon marked the beginning of classical music self-taught with the radio as mentor. So it was no coincidence that on December 7, 1941, she was crouched in a corner by the fireplace listening to the New York Philharmonic when the music stopped with "We interrupt this broadcast to report that Pearl Harbor was bombed by the Japanese this morning. I repeat—"

Deborah did not hear the closing movement of Beethoven's Fifth. She ran into the dining room where the family was finishing the last crumbs of the Lady Baltimore cake. "We're at war. Pearl Harbor's been bombed. I heard it on the radio."

"Don't pay any attention to her," Gamin laughed. "She's always making up stories." What Gamin was paying attention to was his young bride, Sarah. They had been married by a Justice of the Peace in Georgetown and after one night in the local hotel, where Gamin had splurged all the money he could beg or borrow, had continued his honeymoon in the family's company room off the parlor. Jacob Jernigan, just home from preaching at his little church, rose from the table and pushed his plate aside. He had narrowly escaped going to World War I, having just passed his medical exam when the Armistice was signed. Such news was no laughing matter. He knew that Deborah was capable of inventiveness but doubted her prevaricating about such serious matters. Together they dialed WWL, the strongest daytime station.

It was true. Jacob Jernigan fell to his knees and with one arm around his thirteen-year-old daughter prayed humbly, "Lord Jesus, be with us at this hour." Deborah found herself willingly dropping onto her knees by her father. It was a special moment like the time when he confided in her his pride in the purchase of new land. She would remember Pearl Harbor for many reasons: It marked the beginning of terrible years when the family would gather nightly to listen to the priestly doleful voice of Gabriel Heeter, announcing the latest victory or body counts in the sands of Iwo Jima or on the beaches of Normandy. She would remember the star on the field of blue which hung in the parlor window for Gamin, now a soldier smart enough to rise from the rank of the lowly private to sergeant in a matter of weeks. Most of all she would remember Jacob Jernigan, the peacemaker with his "Tut-Tut," who like the Jacob of old pleaded with his God on that December afternoon. The weight of his simple words stirred her as Sunday platitudes never had. At the same time she tasted real fear. In the past she had mentally envisioned Trojan against Greek, Englishmen against Frenchmen, and she had listened to Grandpa recount the atrocities of that bastard Sherman and could almost smell the burning timbers of her great-grandfather's house. But she was not living then. These accounts belonged somewhere in the realm of the stories that came spontaneously from her head. But this was real war, not just a page in history or a battle recreated by Tolstoy. She wanted desperately to join her father in prayer, but she couldn't find the right words and if she could, she was afraid Daddy would interpret her prayer as a commitment and a profession of faith and that she would be forced to make a public statement at the next revival, a prerequisite for baptism and joining the church. So her lips remained silent, but her long, slender fingers intertwined his short, stubby ones. Regaining her composure, she quipped as she often had in the past, "Daddy, do you think my fingers will ever be as big as yours?" Fearful of the consequences, she had deliberately fractured a sacred moment with feigned humor. It was a trick she would often use that closed doors abruptly.

Jacob Jernigan patted his daughter on the head and, undoubtedly thinking her too young to understand, said, "Your hands are like your mother's were when I married her. She was the prettiest bride that ever came to Mount Tabor. She loves you better than anything in the world. She suffered death for you." His words conveyed the gentle reprimand. He remembered the burning of the doll; he had observed the spurned caresses and the open hostility when the hated kneesocks remained a part of Deborah's school wardrobe. He had not interfered; a child's clothes were the wife's province. Besides, his peaceful nature avoided war at any cost. Therefore, a pacifist at heart, Jacob Jernigan, unlike his neighbors, responded to Pearl Harbor with sadness and silence. Absent were the anger and the sudden surge of patriotism that drove young men to the recruiting stations. But Deborah, on that Monday morning when the school assembled in the auditorium to hear President Roosevelt's declaration of war to Congress, could not decide whether the thrill that she experienced with the words "a day that will live in infamy" was the response of a patriotic American or of a lover of words reacting to the magical sound of the phrase spoken so stirringly by the man who had become a hero in the South.

That night, as she snuggled under the mound of quilts and stared into the cold darkness of her room, she could not bring Marlene into focus. A real war would be fought by people whom she knew—real blood would be spilled. She adjusted the soft pad Beryl had given her. Just today she had drawn it from its hiding place. A curious coincidence, she mused. War and womanhood on the same day. No wonder Marlene had disappeared.

CHAPTER

Eight

VALEDICTORY

T he New Year after Pearl Harbor was Janus-eyed. Mount Tabor looked backward to the time when its peaceful hamlet lay down to sleep at night, its dreams undisturbed by the Kamikaze or Gestapo. In those pre-war years, the South at last rallied from the great defeat by those devils in blue and from the Depression where money was scarce as hens' teeth, but whose rich earth and hard work had kept the larder full. The farmer had also found extra compensation by dividing his work between the farm and the new industry, giving Dixie another label—the New South. Robert, Beryl's husband, had found employment in the new paper mill in Georgetown and had risen phenomenally from minimum wage to foreman. Jacob was proud of his son-in-law's enterprise and cut off forty acres of woodland to encourage Robert to keep at least an occasional hand in the soil. According to Jacob, machinery was the devil's workshop, but the good earth kept its tillers away from the sins in the city. Deborah, feeling a far greater attraction to the Cities of the Plain and what temptations they might offer, had visited Beryl in town and seen *Gone with the Wind* and, like Scarlet, had fallen madly in love with Ashley Wilkes, the personification of honor and integrity, and gloried in Scarlet's spirit in her swan song, "Tomorrow is another day." This bravado Deborah demonstrated by defying family coiffures. The newfangled bob she sported was the result of being hooked to an electric machine which dangled hot metal clamps designed to transform straight tresses to frizzes. Anchored under one of these iron tarantulas during a thunderstorm, Deborah came close to repenting, confessing her sins, and joining the church.

Science had also poked its nose into the constituency of Mount Tabor. The new hospital eight miles away had a lucrative business where every married female over thirty submitted to the knife and ever afterward enjoyed sex without fear of pregnancy. Appendectomies were also the rage, and the good surgeon made a million quick and bought a telephone company. Babies now had their birth beds in hospitals and the midwifery business suffered a serious setback.

Deborah would never forget little Robert's advent. Beryl, who had also had an appendectomy even during pregnancy, had been on a strict diet with sweets absolutely forbidden. The afternoon before "the breaking of the water," a phrase whose meaning had escaped the widely read Deborah, Beryl had sat in the dining room before a roaring December fire in the chimney, her sweet tooth aching to be filled with the golden goodness of Mama's sweet potato pudding laced with cinnamon, cloves, and nutmeg. It lay safely out of the reach of buxom Beryl on the top shelf of the corner china cabinet. Little sister, who could make no sense of a doctor's punishing an expectant mother by depriving her taste buds, took the matter into her own hands by scaling the height atop a kitchen stool to fetch a hefty hunk of the delicacies. Dreadful pangs of guilt followed as a result of Beryl's unexpected trip that night to the hospital. Knowing no more than Prissy about birthing a baby, Deborah lay in her bed accusing herself of sororicide and swearing off ever eating another bite of a favorite family dessert. Little Robert, safe and healthy despite the lethal pudding, joined the growing clan of grandchildren, whose parents had followed the biblical dictum, "Be fruitful and multiply." Thus the face of pre-war Mount Tabor turned toward a new year, and Deborah found herself in the seventh grade and about to graduate from grammar school.

Knee-deep-in-stockings, still an oddity, found school neither challenging nor exciting. While the other girls tittered over possibilities of dates, stolen kisses, and "making out," love bumps marred their girlish cheeks. Deborah's face remained free of acne, and if she dreamed of romantic interludes, she did not share them with anyone. What she liked most about school was the library where she could ride with Zane Gray over the purple sage or under the Tonto Rim. *The Bobbsey Twins* was kid stuff, and even Louisa Mae Alcott's women were a little too goody-goody to satisfy her thirst for adventure. The worlds of Eliot, Brontë, and even Shakespeare were not titles on the elementary school bookshelf, but there were several copies of *101 Best Loved Poems of the American People*. So she memorized Longfellow, Holmes, and Bryant and even attempted to write verse herself. Graduation was nearing and it looked as though she would beat her arch rival, Stephanie, as top student despite the B she had made in arithmetic. She and Stephanie had shared a double desk. Each of them at least twice had braced her feet on the opposite row of desks to give the other a not-so-gentle push, which landed a bottom on the well-worn pine floor. Both had reached the age where girls were no longer paddled, and a deprived recess was no punishment for Deborah, who preferred reading to hop scotch and jump rope, anyway. On one such occasion Deborah penned the four rhymed lines of what would be the opening of her valedictory address. She showed her poetic achievement to Miss Davis, her English teacher, who commended her effort and said it was a good start and that there was another kind of poetry which didn't rhyme.

She lent her a copy of *Leaves of Grass*. Indeed, it was different, and although she didn't get the full impact of the poetry, she loved the sound of the words that rolled off her tongue as sonorously as organ notes. Into her hands Miss Davis put Dickinson, Teasdale, and Millay. Deborah decided then and there that she would devote her life to writing poetry and would one day see her name numbered among the best-loved poets of America.

Graduation came at last. For the first time in her years in school, Deborah felt a sense of pride. Valedictorian she was and it was she who would make the speech that marked the termination of elementary school. Knee-deep-in-stockings would wear her first long dress.

Hannah, since the death of Emily, had continued plying her needle for other little girls. Her nimble fingers seemed to move without her eyes, creating delicate rosebuds, filmy tatting, and clusters of French knots pleating baptismal gowns and birthday dresses. Deborah noted the faraway look in her eyes as her hands, now prematurely arthritic, hemstitched a hem, the final touch on her newest creation. Hannah's reading tastes had changed, and although she still read the Bible, the books Deborah often found in her hands were novels of mystery and romance, temporary respites from the visions haunting her. No longer did Deborah resent being called Sister. Perhaps Hannah sensed that Deborah understood her loss.

So it was that Hannah made the graduation gown. It was white voile with a square neck and puff sleeves. The white insertion around the neck, sleeves, and waist was threaded with pink velvet ribbon and tied into baby bows. Different from her classmates' organdies over starched petticoats, Deborah's dress fell in straight soft lines over her thin body. At last she stood among her peers without the excess clothes, the leanest and the tallest. Beryl had washed her hair and given it a lemon rinse that turned the kinky perm into soft curls. Just before she went on stage, Miss Davis rubbed a little tangee natural color on her pale cheeks and lips. Deborah looked at herself in the mirror, drew off her round gold-rimmed glasses, and decided she looked almost pretty despite the protruding teeth. Stephanie's parents had the dentist put braces on her uneven cuspids, but Daddy said if God had meant her teeth to be straight, he would have made them that way. He relented later and Dr. Small eventually gave her an even smile.

They were all there except for Gamin in a training camp in Oklahoma. Jacob and Anna Jernigan had come early to get seats on the front row. They were proud of this miracle child. Although she had none of the domestic skills of her sisters, her nose always poked in a book, Anna thanked God that her attempts to abort this child had failed, and now she was almost as strong as her siblings. Anna gave herself the full credit, remembering the long nights she had held vigil with measles, pneumonia, whooping cough, and diphtheria as well as the forced feedings that kept life flickering in the thin, long frame. What Anna could not understand was the ingratitude and even the streak of cruelty. She would never forget that terrible Christmas and the burning doll, especially the replica of her wedding dress that she had laboriously created in miniature. And Jacob hadn't even chastised the child. What was wrong with a child who beamed all her affection on a father who had never experienced the agony of child-bearing and whose paternal duties did not include twenty-four hour nursing shifts? Well, now that Deborah had finished seventh grade, Anna had decided she would not encourage her to continue school. It was time to teach her housework, now that the others had married and her own health was failing. It was time for Deborah to understand the sacrifices that her mother had made for her. She had wrecked her health for this thankless child. Modern surgery had done nothing for migraines, hot flashes, and arthritis, and Deborah Jernigan had shown more love to a coal black than she had to her own mother.

Jacob Jernigan had other thoughts, quite different from those of his wife. He, too, had felt the sting of Deborah's rejection. Of all his children she alone had failed to make a commitment to his God. He thought she had read too many worldly books which had nothing to do with repentance and baptism. Yet he loved her in a different way from the affection he had for each of his other children. At odd moments he had felt a closeness that he shared with no one else. Deborah understood his passion for the land, his discomfort with Anna's ill health, and her constant nagging over something so trivial as lingering too long after church—Jacob never saw a stranger and loved to talk—or whether they could afford a new car or still carry on the store books those who had failed to pay last year's grocery bill. Generosity and its twin, kindness, had rendered him love and respect from white and colored. Mr. Jacob was a man who kept his word and would accommodate anyone down-and-out. Why, didn't he return the stolen groceries from his store after the sheriff had found them in the Shelleys' house? Anna's scathing tongue did not commend such benevolence, but Deborah had secretly hugged him and whispered, "Daddy, it's too bad the church does not beatify Old Testament patriarchs. You would be Saint Jacob." Where in the world did his child get such big words? When he remembered, he put the accent on the first syllable of her name. When he made a mistake, Deborah always giggled. Pronunciation of her name had become a secret joke between them as had his short grace when he was in a hurry. "Thank the Lord, what we got, Christ's sake, Amen." Once she had playfully reprimanded him for such an abbreviated, irreverent blessing, particularly after Mama had slaved over a hot stove. Thereafter, laughter had punctuated his prayer at table. He worried about the relationship between mother and daughter, but his gentle counseling had not produced the desired results. He felt the unhappiness of both and sensed that one day he would have to take sides. In the meantime, he would simply enjoy this funny little girl whose head was somewhere in the clouds even as her feet were planted firmly on the ground. She was a dreamer who knew where she was going.

The lights in the gym dimmed and an outside spotlight picked up Mrs. Rhea's Glee Club girls. They were singing Handel's "Largo." Deborah had heard *The Messiah* one Easter Sunday on the radio. Now she listened to the words: "Father, in heaven, thy children hear." How beautiful, she thought! What a difference between the songs sung in church. "There is a fountain filled with blood, drawn from Emmanuel's veins." The metaphor was grotesque. She couldn't imagine God being hooked up to a needle and connected to a fountain from which his blood flowed. But these words in the "Largo." They signified a loving relationship between father and children—a father, although holy and supreme, who loved unconditionally with no strings attached except the return of his love with trust. Deborah looked down to the front row of seats and spotted Jacob Jernigan's bald head. Her throat tightened. She was afraid she was going to cry. The speech she had prepared was original, not copied from the book Miss Davis had given her. It began with her quatrain:

> *Once when we were very small*
> *We took a step and did not fall;*
> *Step by step we've come from there*
> *To our seventh grade graduation year.*

Deborah remembered that first day in school when she, indeed, had fallen and the humiliation that had followed. She wondered if Miss Agatha were sitting somewhere in the audience. Too bad that she could not see the smirk hovering around Knee-deep-in-stockings' mouth.

> *Teachers, parents, friends, and classmates,*
> *A great English writer, John Donne, wrote a poem*
> *"A Valediction: Forbidding Mourning."*
> *The writer was about to take a dangerous trip on the continent in 1611.*
> *He was telling his wife not to grieve for him while he was away, because love grew stronger with separation.*
> *Our class tonight is also about to take a trip that will*

*take us in many directions. We may never again be as-
sembled as we are now. Like John Donne, I also forbid
you to mourn. For what we have learned, we are grateful
to our parents who sent us here and our teachers who
have taught us. But a tearful farewell to grammar school
seems inappropriate as we look forward to other classrooms, new friends, other opportunities. "Good-bye" is
such a sad word.*

Let us say instead, "Hello."

She made her curtsy. This was supposed to be the end of
her speech. Suddenly she saw the bright silver dollars—seven of
them—one for each grade in school—pasted on a congratulation
card and signed "Daddy." It would please him if she mentioned
God in the end. At least she could say the motto on the silver dollars. After all, it was a simple thing to do to please somebody.

The words came out in almost a whisper. "In God we trust."
Daddy heard her. His response was as resonant as hers was soft.
Never before—not even cheers for basketball games—had anything sounded so loud. "Hallelujah! Praise God!" Then came the
laughter which got louder and louder, atoms of laughter crashing
against the walls and bouncing around the bleachers. Deborah
shrank into the pristine whiteness of her long gown with baby
pink bows and wished with all her soul that she could have been
the infant in a white shroud who failed to give the first whimper
on Aunt Phoenix's ample knee and who had floated up on a
cloud on a mountain where no one could see her or touch her.

CHAPTER

Nine

GRANDMA JERNIGAN

Grandma Jernigan, who had proclaimed Deborah dead at birth and had called her such an "ugly little thing" was certainly not born dead nor near death any one of her ninety-nine years. One night she slipped quietly away in her sleep, possessing all of her teeth with never a scar by a surgeon's hand marring her slight frame whose weight never tipped the hundred mark. Grandma lived a five-minute stroll from Deborah's house, but on dark nights Deborah could make it in three minutes. Deborah, who had heard the story of the dire pronouncement she had made at her granddaughter's birth, took great satisfaction in teasing the old lady and showing off her precocity with her stories, giving her the lie of an earlier judgment. Her granddaughter's learning did not impress her. The things about which Deborah prattled were as useless to Grandma Jernigan as putting a rock in a hole and expecting a turnip to sprout. What did she care about Hannibal crossing the Alps or Saladin conquering Jerusalem? What was important were the tiny scraps that she pieced together and made into squares that eventually became a quilt. The finished product had value; it would help keep out the cold on winter nights after the last oak log had fallen into dying embers in the chimney. What did Jane Eyre know about trouble? Why she had had sixteen younguns to the time—a set of twins plus a set of triplets—and had survived her husband who had died of dropsy in his forties. Tiring Grandma with her stories, Deborah would frequently probe her about the past.

"Grandma, when did you first kiss Grandpa?" On hearing the question, suddenly the blue eyes came alive illumined by an inner light, and the pleated lips formed a coy smile that transformed a face seamed with wrinkles into that of a girl.

"Taint none of your business. Ain't you shame asking such questions? You ought to be home helping your Mama. She done spoiled you rotten. Your sisters had to work. Anna's got one child left home and she ain't good for nothing." The words were not really a reprimand. Deborah's sharp eyes had evaluated the change of expression that invited more questions.

"Grandma, what color was your hair?" Deborah gently lifted the bonnet from her head. Her sparse gray hair was drawn back to the nape of her neck in a ball the size of a large hen's egg. Deborah's long, thin fingers wrested a single strand from its tight enclosure. "Were you pretty, Grandma?"

"Pretty is as pretty does." Her fingers unwound the ball and twisted it back, intact with the stray tress. "My hair was about the color of yours. It was long. Sitting in a chair like this, it touched the floor. Your grandpa used to part it in half and cross it over my bosom." There was slight reddening of the sallow cheeks that Deborah did not miss.

"Were you in bed? Naked, Grandma?"

"Shut your mouth, girl. You got some nerve. Ain't nothing you afraid to ask. Ain't nothing you afraid to do. If you'd been my youngun, I'd put the strap to you when you cut your hair."

"Daddy says I got a lot of you in me. He says you stole grandpa right out of the arms of a rich girl who could have added two big farms to the Jernigan land. Come on, Grandma. Tell me about it. I won't tell a soul. Except one day, I might write about it. Not using your real name, of course."

Deborah eased herself down on the floor at her knees, put her granny's bonnet on her own head, and tied the strings in a bow under her chin. The old rocker upon which Grandma was sitting on the front porch that October afternoon was smaller than the others there. Her husband's hands had crafted it especially for her. The sturdy oak wood had a natural soft sheen that had known neither wax nor polish. Maybe she could write a poem about it, Deborah thought. Sturdy with a soft inner glow. Like the old woman in front of her whose hands were busy fitting a hexagonal red scrap with red dots to a solid blue circle. The space between was miniscule. Already the quilt maker was scanning just the right filler that would be cut to size—an odd shape of no geometric pattern—unique among its squared, angled, and rounded community.

Never lifting her eyes to her granddaughter, she began: "The Scots, my folks, was pore as church mice. My Pa he got killed in the war. That was before I was born."

"There's a word for that, granny. You were born posthumously. Like David Copperfield. Did you have a caul over your head? It's supposed to give you special powers. Live a long time. Be good and sweet like you," Deborah flattered.

"Humph! Ain't nobody called me sweet since Dan'l. I had it hard like my Ma. After Pa died in the war—we don't even know where he was buried, up north somewheres—we had to move in with old Ma. She was as mean as a snake. She didn't want me and my two brothers, Monk and Charlie. Four extra mouths to feed, she said. Sides old Pa wasn't no kind of provider. He worked turpentine all week, took his pay, grabbed a fishing pole, a half-gallon of corn liquor, and headed for the Big Pee Dee. We didn't see hide nor hair of him until Sunday night about sundown. He'd come staggering in and crawl in the bed on top of Old Ma's quilt. You could hear him snoring to the road." Suddenly laughter rippled her throat and shook her whole body. She dropped her sewing and looked toward the chinaberry tree and beyond.

"What's funny, Grandma?"

She lifted the coffee can beside the rocker and spat a smart tingle on the tin. When Granny got started on a story, Deborah didn't even mind the snuff. Besides, she never drooled and the Sweet Society powder remained tucked between her lower lip and teeth. In fact, Deborah had fetched her a box from the store. The dime was in her pocket.

"One Sunday night Old Pa was snoring away—dead to the world. Old Ma took her quilting needle—the big one she used to tack the quilt to the frame before she had the quilting bee—and sewed him up with tobacco twine from the top of his head to the soles of his feet. She took a tobacco stick—you know the kind you string tobacco on before it is put in the barn to be cured—and give him the whipping of his life. You could hear his cussing and hollering a mile down the road. After that he didn't touch a drop for nigh on to two months. But that whipping cured him of messing up Old Ma's quilts. Didn't cure him of drinking though. Took the Grim Reaper to cure that. He fell in the river dead drunk and drowned. Was a good swimmer, though. Maybe he just got plain tired of Old Ma's sharp tongue and all the hungry mouths to feed." She bit off a length of thread and proceeded to refurbish her needle.

"Did Old Ma cry?"

"Course she did. It would of been the scandal of the county if she hadn't. She wrung her hands and said she reckoned we'd all starve to death. The more she hollered the more vittles was brought in. We had sacks of sweet potatoes and Irish ones, too. The neighbors come bringing corn meal and grits ground at old man Pope's mill. There was a whole keg of ribbon cane syrup and a fifty-pound sack of sugar. There was so many bags of rice that lasted so long that the weevils got in it. Best thing Old Pa could have done for the family was to drown himself. I kind of felt sorry for him. I druther be dead than live with Old Ma. Even when we had all that pile of rations, Old Ma would put the smallest helpings on our plates. Now Monk and Charlie, soon as she got out of the kitchen, they knowed where she hid the leftover taters. There wouldn't be a one left for breakfast. Old Ma tried to put Old Pa's razor strop to us. But my Mama had spunk. She dared her to touch one of us. She threatened to go tell old man Henry Tindall that Old Ma was cutting wood off his place. Mama was the only child Old Ma and Old Pa had. Reckon with all the fighting they didn't have much time for loving."

"But Granny, what did your mama do? How did she support you?"

"Well, Old Ma give us a roof over our heads, such as it was. One time it snowed and I woke up with the snow all over my bed. Old Ma had patched the roof until it wasn't nothing but patches. But Mama, she worked in the fields, chopping cotton, stripping fodder, hoeing corn. At night she sewed. She was right handy with the needle. She made Miss Ellen's children's school clothes and a lot of their Sunday dresses. They was two spoiled younguns. Never did a lick of work. Only had to set up and look pretty in their smocked blouses and jumpers that Mama made them. Miss Ellen taught school before she married Mr. Bob. They wouldn't let married women teach. Mr. Bob had the biggest farm around and acres and acres of the finest timber in the county. Both girls got anything they wanted. A new coat every year—trips to Charleston. Sally Maud and Gertrude. 'Cept Sally Maud didn't get Dan'l."

"Oh, Granny, tell me about that!"

Once again she stopped her sewing and shook her bowed head over the multicolored scraps in her lap. Deborah had heard that Grandma never cried, not even when her oldest son got run over by a train. Searching her face intently, Deborah could have sworn she saw tears glimmer in her deep-set blue eyes. Her voice, however, did not betray emotion.

"I was just sixteen when I went to a Sunday school convention at Little Bethel. It was a singing get—together and all the churches from miles around came. Mama had made me a red gingham dress with a flounced skirt. I had a sash made out of a solid red color tied in a big bow in the back. I reckon my waist wasn't more than eighteen inches."

Just like Scarlet, Deborah thought. "Did you have a big bosom?"

Granny gave her a stern look. That part of the anatomy ladies did not discuss. "You could tell I was a woman alright. Mama had my hair all done up fancy with a red ribbon. Made me look taller than I was. Anyhow, Dan'l Jernigan had come from Mount Tabor. He played the guitar and could sing so good that it would make the hair rise straight up on your head. I ain't never gonna forget what he sung. 'In the sweet by and by. We shall meet on that beautiful shore.' I heard that he had been keeping company with Sally Maud. Anyway, she was right at his elbow and clapped longer and louder than anybody else. Sometime in the middle of that song, he seen me and smiled. Every time he would get to 'we shall meet on that beautiful shore,' he would look at me. Between the verses as he strummed on his guitar, he winked at me. My heart was beating so loud I was afraid it would show through my dress."

Deborah's brown eyes widened. She grasped her granny's hand and whispered. "What happened, Granny?"

"That's for me to know and for you to find out," she finished. Unclasping her granddaughter's hand, she folded her unfinished square and dropped it in the sewing basket. "It's time for me to feed my chickens," she said. Like Scheherazade, she left her listener agape and disappeared into the house.

CHAPTER

Ten

THE WAR YEARS

Years afterward, high school and World War II remained linked events for Deborah. While she traveled vicariously nightly by radio from Normandy to the South African desert, her wars were fought without a grenade or rifle. Her weapon was the silent determination that one day she would see beyond the flat land of Mount Tabor and glimpse Canaan, making her exodus, as did the other Jernigan children, into biblical land flowing with milk and honey. The metaphor did not appeal to her so she rapidly substituted champagne and caviar, neither of which she had ever tasted.

Autumn was the season of the dreaded revivals. They arrived annually after the corn was harvested, the tobacco marketed, the cotton ginned and baled; but before the debts incurred during the previous year were settled. A bountiful harvest was a rarity and a blessing sent down from heaven. Often drought or flood destroyed entire crops. Deborah wondered what happened to the benevolent powers above during the lean years. Nevertheless, in plenty or want, come October Mount Tabor Baptist hosted the protracted meetings led by fiery evangelists, eager to convert sinners but also to line their wallets from money crops. They came from "over the river," meaning the Carolina tidewaters, or "upstate" meaning such faraway places as Spartanburg, South Carolina, or Hickory, North Carolina. The Jernigan household provided room and board for the good preacher, who set up headquarters in the company room reserved for holy folk. They came in all sizes and shapes, each possessing an enormous appetite apparent in his girth. They feasted on Anna's fried chicken and coconut custard pie and drank gallons of iced tea even though sugar was rationed. Deborah suspected that the blind piano player imbibed in stronger refreshments just before the nightly service because as he gave her an avuncular blind pat on her bosom, she caught an aroma resembling neither orange pekoe tea nor chicory coffee. At any rate she was indebted to the blind slightly tipsy musician who came down from the pulpit after his invitation to the sinners to give a rousing rendition of the altar call song, "Just as I Am without One Plea." Deborah was one of the prized converts that each revivalist would like to claim, she being the only one of Brother Jacob's children who had not made a profession of faith. The unsaved Deborah was not about to confess her sins to Mount Tabor's ears, even though she had been threatened with the possibility that lightning might strike her dead before next fall. One night lightning did strike her in the form of an idea. What if she learned to play the piano to summon other mourners to the mercy seat? Then she would not be expected to break her musical invitation. The Jernigan parlor had both an upright piano and a pedal organ. Both of her brothers and two of her sisters had learned to play by ear, Lily being so talented that she could play any song in multiple keys. Deborah had no such ear, but she knew she could learn to read notes. The problem was a teacher. So after one such unsettling fall when again Deborah was not numbered with the new "saved ones," she decided to broach the subject of lessons with Jacob and employ her "artful strategy" that she hoped would result in her becoming the "artful dodger" of the annual altar calls.

Daddy had just returned from his little church where he spent each weekend with his flock. Sunday afternoon would bring him home in his rattling Ford with no prospect of a new one in wartime. Often he had a flat tire, which he repaired with the aid of resinous rubber patches and an air pump. Today, as he emerged from the car, his coat on one arm with his hand clutching the Bible, Deborah met him on the front steps. Pressing her cheek against his wilted starched shirt damp with perspiration, she gave him a quick hug and led him to one of the green rocking chairs that lined the wide front porch. What she had to say was not for Mama's ears.

"I'm so glad you're home, Daddy." Although this was the preamble to her ruse, Deborah actually spoke truth. Jacob's daughter felt more secure when her father was at home. There was a kind of strength and reassurance that seemed to flow from his sturdy hands and his strong embrace. The word *love* she had never voiced. It was a word that some poet had said that when it was too often used, the user profaned it. Even now, she dared not use it to manipulate. Someday she would voice it or attempt to write it. Someday, perhaps, there might be, if she were lucky, another person to whom she could not only say the word but also give it without fear or reservation. Such were dreams that she shared with no one except in imaginary dialogs on sleepless nights when she sensed the vastness of the midnight and the awful press of stars.

"De-'Borah, how was church?" She knew what was behind that question. He was kind enough not to ask if she had finally made a commitment.

"Oh, Preacher Stone seemed happy. With the collection today he went away with over five hundred dollars. Not small change for a week with free room and board. Oh, and you know

Ben Hiller, who got saved Wednesday night? He got drunk Friday night and gave his wife, Martha, a black eye. Somebody said he was back in jail. He'll have a whole bushel of sins to confess next year. I'm sorry, Daddy. No, I didn't go to the altar. I read that in some churches everybody confesses together from a form prayer. Anyway, if Jesus is our only mediator, why does everybody have to hear?" Once again she had used holy writ to drive a point home.

He laughed in spite of himself. "You too smart for your own good. I just hope you can argue your way by St. Peter. De-'Borah, I believe God has a special mission for you. Don't make fun of God's children. Plenty of people hold to their faith. Ben Hiller is just one of those weak souls who can't bear up under temptation. Honey, I want you to find the faith that I have. It will keep you going, even in dark places."

"Daddy, I thought of a way I could serve God. If I could have music lessons and learn to read notes, I could play for church. I could play new hymns that we don't know."

"You know I don't have the money or the time to take you to a music teacher. It's all I can do to make ends meet. And De-'Borah, I hope I can discover a way to send you to college."

"Oh, Daddy!" The words came spontaneously at the sound of college. "I love you more than anybody. But I found an ad about music lessons through the mail. The American College of Music. I could pay for them with my money I get working in tobacco. They even send you tests through the mail."

A month later, Deborah Jernigan sat in front of the piano in the unheated parlor and learned from her first lesson the treble notes and played her first scale in C major. By spring she was playing hymns, and although her fingering would have given a teacher a heart attack, and the pedaling used as the spirit moved would have guaranteed the demise of a musical pedagogue, she was soon to be the official pianist at Mount Tabor. As the lessons advanced, she played pieces from the masters, not after the manner of Rubenstein but after the manner of one who had not only escaped the horrors of revival but was also thrilling to the counting of notes of simple Beethoven and Schubert. One day she found Jacob's Masonic manual, which she read voraciously, hoping desperately to discover the secret of the order. She was disappointed to find that "it is too sacred to be written," but she amazed Jacob Jernigan when he heard her playing the Masonic hymn.

"De-'Borah" he questioned, "where did you find that?"

Impishly she held up the little black book bound in leather and lisped the words from the text, "So mote it be."

CHAPTER

Eleven

RUPERT

A certain mystery surrounded Rupert, who had suddenly appeared in Big Joe and Maggie Poston's house, which squatted among a forest of oak and saplings interspersed with stumps. The lumber from their trees had been transformed into hardwood floors and Early American furniture. Three miles from the main road that ran through Mount Tabor down a dirt lane rutted by the wheels of trucks sagging under the weight of pulp wood or virgin pine, the tow-headed big-eared Rupert had traversed to join the heretofore childless couple. Big Joe needed an heir as well as another pair of hands to slop the pigs, stake the cow, chop firewood, draw washing water from the well, and eventually man a saw at the Poston mill. How Big Joe found him and adopted him no one knew.

One didn't question Big Joe because it was because he weighed nigh on to three hundred pounds and could flatten

77

an adversary with a mere punch of his left paw or because everyone knew that Big Joe feared neither God nor man. No one questioned him when the body of Billy Bob Leggett, a colored man who dared to sass Big Joe over wages, was found one Sunday morning with a rope around his neck less than a mile from Big Joe's sawmill. Billy Bob's demise evoked no open discussion among white or black, the former knowing there would come no justice from the law and the latter fearing the hooded white-clad men who sometimes gathered on moonless nights and processed down the road waving flaming torches. Most repeated the unlikely story that Billy Bob had drunk too much moonshine after payday and had hanged himself because his sweetie had run off with his first cousin. Deborah Jernigan was brazen enough to say to Jacob, "Anybody believing that story has got to be retarded. Daddy, why don't you do something about it?"

Jacob Jernigan shook his bald head. "I learned a long time ago what you can't do anything about, you may as well as let it alone."

"But that's not right," Deborah raged. "Big Joe ought to be in jail along with those sons of bitches that helped him."

"Deborah Jernigan, where did you learn such words?"

Ignoring Jacob's reprimand, she rushed on. "Isn't it because Billy Bob had black skin? What would Jesus say or does he care for only those white sheep like the ones on our Sunday school cards?" Her words were scathing. Jacob dropped his head and forgot to pursue admonition against the forbidden epithet.

Rupert, however, never saw one of those Good Shepherd cards because the Postons worked seven days a week, curing tobacco on Sunday and never shutting down the sawmill unless it broke on its own accord. Rupert's catechism was work without ceasing, speak only when questioned, and face the strap without flinching. Perhaps mastery of these precepts and submission to Big Joe's enslavement carried the promise that one day Rupert would be Lord of the Poston lands. Rupert, whose muscles hardened with drudgery, remained a shrimp of a little fellow despite

Maggie's ample table of cornbread, pork belly, and collard greens. Big Joe had certainly made a mistake by not inquiring in that orphanage, which everyone supposed was Rupert's first home, about the dimensions of his ancestry. On the rare occasions when Rupert accompanied his adopted father to the Jernigan store to fill up his log truck with gasoline or to replenish the supply of Prince Albert tobacco, Big Joe was never heard to address Rupert by his Christian name nor the affectionate *son*. He was simply *boy* or *you there*, making him as anonymous as a single leaf among April leaves.

Rupert was older than Deborah, the age of her brother Gamin, but having failed two grades, was still in grammar school. From the beginning she felt a kinship with the boy with the floppy ears who on some mornings met the bus at the crossroads, but on many others hid in the dense undergrowth of brush and fallen timbers, preferring to lie around until school was out to being the object of ridicule by his peers who had christened him "Jackass" because of his big ears and apparent lack of mental acuity. One morning Mr. Joseph, the bus driver, suspecting that Rupert was somewhere crouching among the spring foliage of sweet gum and huckleberry bushes, got out of the bus and, facing the road leading to the Postons, yelled, "Come out, Rupert. I see you." To the delight of twenty-odd schoolmates, Rupert crawled out from the bushes and boarded the bus, picking off the pine burrs clinging to his blue denim overalls. Deborah was the only one who did not laugh. Instead, she motioned the reluctant scholar, "creeping like snail unwillingly to school," to the empty seat usually occupied by Cousin Vernie, absent that morning because of a trip with her Mama to Georgetown to buy an Easter frock. "Rupert," she whispered, as the bus changed to second gear and sputtered forward, "I hate school, too."

This was the remark that began the tacit friendship. They spoke very little at recess. Rupert and Deborah, the loners, went their separate ways. At some point the shrimp shot up to a gangly youth, and his voice changed to a manly bass, not unpleasant

79

to the ear. About the same time, he dropped out of school and Deborah's contact with him was rare. Once she saw him across the street from the drugstore in Big Joe's red pickup in town, loading sacks of fertilizer from Brown's Feed and Seed Store. They waved at each other, and she could imagine that his smile matched hers.

To the surprise of everyone in Mount Tabor, Rupert Poston was the first to be inducted in the army. Big Joe said he was drafted, but Mount Tabor gossip was that at last Rupert had found his way out of the morass and was happy to exchange Big Joe's denim for Uncle Sam's khaki.

It was a cool Sunday afternoon in October. The sun cast those special golden glints of light, harbingers of winter. Fifteen-year-old Deborah sat at the piano practicing her first minor scale, following the instructions in the mail order manual. Her keen ear picked up the oddity as the note deviated from the major scale. What she heard she liked, and she toyed idly with the idea that perhaps minor scales represented a step up from the regular, the mundane of the humdrum existence of every day. Recently she had heard snatches of Bach's B minor mass on the radio. One day she would listen to it in its entirety. It might be through music, as she had ironically suggested to her father earlier, that she would grasp the meaning of *Communion*. She liked the Catholic word *Mass*. In these meanderings accompanied by her occasional trilling notes on the scale not written in her exercise, she did not hear the front screen door open nor Anna's "Come in, Rupert."

At her elbow stood a tall soldier. He stood twirling his trench cap. His hair, having outgrown the GI cut, was parted on the side and lay neatly in undefined crimps above the ears that now did not seem so prominent. On the sleeve of his coat between the elbow and shoulder were three triangular stripes. Cross sables and brass buttons decorated the lapels. There was a moment of awkward silence. Then snapping himself to attention and saluting smartly, he said, "Sergeant Poston reporting, Miss Jernigan."

"Why, Rupert Poston," she gasped. The man in front of her

80

fingering his cap and looking at her uncertainly held no resemblance to the "Jackass" who had crawled out of the bushes and shamefacedly boarded the bus. Gone was "Boy" shambling behind Big Joe. She addressed him by his full name befitting his new identity and independence. Nicknames and diminutives were so demeaning, she had so often thought, and her own name shortened to Deb sounded like somebody who couldn't pronounce or spell *debutante*.

For one of the first times in her life, Deborah Jernigan was at a loss for words. Aside from the fact that social amenities with Rupert had been rare and confined to brief hellos and smiles, she suddenly realized that this was the first time that a boy had come to see her. But the young man who stood before her in his tailored green uniform was no boy. Unconsciously she smoothed back her hair as her feet groped for her shoes lying near the piano pedals.

"Deborah, I kind of wanted to see you before leaving. My unit will be going overseas when I get back. Don't know whether I'll be going after them Nazis or snagging the Japs. Kind of hope it will be Europe. I might be lucky enough to get a look at one of those French girls." A blush crept up his cheeks suffusing his whole face. No longer the confident soldier, he shifted from one foot to the other and studied the yellow rose design in the cushion of the mohair chair beside the piano.

"Oh, Rupert, I'm so proud of you. Why you've already made sergeant! You must be some smart guy." Reaching out to his hand, she led him to the nearby sofa. "I guess you showed Mount Tabor. I bet you'll be an officer by the time the war is over."

A smile broadened his face. She noticed that his eyes were very blue and that his lashes were uncommonly long for a man. There was a certain strength in the set of his smooth-shaven jaw. Suddenly she wanted to touch his face and take a deep look into those blue pools that now glinted with the pleasure of her compliment.

"No, Deborah. The army doesn't work like that. You have to

go to school. But I'm going to apply for OCS. Reckon it won't be easy. But I wanted you to know I got my high school diploma. I went to night school while I was in training. You being so smart, I kind of thought you would like to know. Also, I kind of wanted to say good-bye. Guess I wanted you to wish me luck. Maybe write to me sometime. I could write back. Course, I can't write and spell as good as you."

Years later, Deborah couldn't account for what happened next. She found her arms around his neck and her cheek pressed against his. "Oh, Rupert, I will write to you. Every week. I don't care about your spelling. Just tell me everything. Where you are. What you're thinking."

It was her first kiss and one that she would remember always. Knee-deep-in-stockings and Jackass had become Deborah Jernigan and Rupert Poston, no longer misfits but two young people brought together for a brief moment, sharing wordlessly the loneliness of the past. How strange, she would muse, that war had brought about their oneness, and however ephemeral it might be, it was a moment to be brought out in other lonely hours and relived. It would remain forever nameless—too sacred like Jacob Jernigan's secret order to be written or uttered to alien ears.

"Deborah Jernigan." It was Anna's voice. Something must have stopped the words that Deborah expected to come from her mother. A miracle, she thought afterward. Was it an invisible hand that had clamped her mother's lips and silenced her sharp tongue, or was it a memory buried for years of another kiss—sweet, sad, and not lasting? At any rate there was an opening of a door left slightly ajar, a crack in a wall through which mother and daughter had a brief glimpse into each other and discovered a marked resemblance.

Rupert was on his feet. "I'm just going, Miz Jernigan." He was already at the door. Deborah heard the screen door close softly and watched the soldier, now capped, stride down the walk and to the red pickup. As the engine died down the road, Deborah turned to the figure still standing in the doorway. "Thank you,

Mother." She had never used that address before. She turned to the piano and began practicing the simple major scales.

In the months ahead, there were several letters from Sgt. Poston, surprisingly well written. The first awkwardly thanked her for the letter he had received. Later his missives described the heat of the desert, the roar of aircraft, the sad notes of reveille, the half-naked natives. Once he mentioned the good-bye kiss from a certain smart young girl and wondered if he might expect a second one to welcome him home. The latter was said jestingly with no trace of nostalgia for Mount Tabor staining his words. Instead, it seemed to Deborah, a certain mist hovered over his letters, threatening to burst into a shower revealing a loneliness had the climate permitted a longer season. But suddenly the letters stopped. Months passed and victory and the return of soldiers. The stars in windows signifying a son in service disappeared and former GI's enrolled in schools sponsored by Uncle Sam.

"Well, poor boy," Jacob Jernigan said one night at the supper table. "He never knew anything but hard work and no thanks. Big Joe says he's heard nothing from him. Army hasn't even notified him that he's missing in action. Big Joe says he'll have to wait ten years to collect the ten thousand dollars due him. Reckon Rupert never even had a sweetheart as far as I know." He helped himself to another spoonful of grits to accompany the last slice of country ham swimming in red-eye gravy.

Deborah's eyes met her mother's. On the shelf in her bedroom there was an anthology of British poetry. One of the selections was a sonnet by a young soldier written before he was killed in World War I. In it he described the poignant farewell to his sweetheart before he left for the front. Deborah had memorized the lines. As the conversation turned from "poor Rupert" to the prospects of an early freeze and the first hog killing of the season, Deborah listened to the voice of Rupert Brooke:

The Hill

Breathless, we flung us on the windy hill,
Laughed in the sun, and kissed the lovely grass.
You said, "Through glory and ecstasy we pass;
Wind, sun, and earth remain, the birds sing still,
When we are old, are old...." "And when we die
All's over that is ours; and life burns on
Through other lovers, other lips," said I,
—"Heart of my heart, our heaven is now, is won!"

"We are earth's best that learnt her lesson here.
Life is our cry. We have kept the faith!" we said;
"We shall go down with unreluctant tread
Rose-crowned into the darkness!"...Proud we were,
And laughed, that had such brave true things to say.
—And then you suddenly cried, and turned away.

CHAPTER

Twelve

SINS OF THE FLESH

Such words as *masturbation*, *lesbian*, and *gay* had not yet made their entrance into Mount Tabor's lexicon. It was a euphemistic society. "Falling off the roof" substituted for menstruation; a "woods colt" was a bastard; one who had "dropped her candy" was an unwed mother; while *queer* covered a multitude of odd people not talked about in polite society. *Conjugation*, to Deborah, meant the declension of verbs in the indicative, subjunctive, and imperative moods, and *congress* was a two-body legislature elected by the people and sent to Washington where they came back richer each election year as they made their rounds at July barbecues, shaking hands with the folks down home and kissing babies whether sweet-smelling or otherwise. Even so, *adultery* was a common word, and every child and adult knew its meaning. It was one of the first four-syllable words heard on Sunday as the preacher intoned the Seventh Commandment. To Deborah the connotation was more fascinating than forbidden. Even in the protected world of Mount Tabor, students had read *The Scarlet Letter* and some had found *Madame Bovary* tucked behind a row of F's in the Georgetown County library, although *Lady Chatterley* was nowhere to be found. Of course, Deborah knew that all the kings of England had committed the dreadful sin and even queens had been beheaded for such an offense. Quite unfair, thought Deborah, who now understood "the double standard." She took comfort in Jesus' preventing the stoning of the woman caught in the act and privately found Mary Magdalene's so-called lurid past more provocative than that of the sinless virgin. Outspoken though she was, Deborah kept such heresies to herself, but was just as intrigued as any Mount Taborite with the stories whispered about Cousin Hester's post-conjugal rendezvous. She alone wondered if the name had destined her third cousin thrice removed by marriage to follow the path of Hawthorne's heroine. She sometimes imagined a scarlet A instead of *Jesus Saves* brandished in a glittering gold letter on Cousin Hester's pristine white blouse which she wore to church on Sunday morning.

Cousin Hester, a native of the Up Country, was married to Cousin Theophila Ard, from Mama's side of the family—an Ichabod Crane in overalls with a straw hat crushing his straw blond curls, usually damp with perspiration. His pale blue eyes seemed to focus without peripheral vision, and his hawk-like nose brooded over a scraggly moustache and sniffed frequently as though he smelled something bad. Deborah was intrigued with his name. The unabridged dictionary at school rendered the "a" ending making it a girl's name. No wonder the high-pitched *whang* of his drawl matched the name so well. Questioning Mama about his predecessors, Deborah learned that Great Cousin Robert, twice-removed, discovered that his daughter, Mary Jane, had "dropped her candy" to a damn piano tuner. A shotgun wedding ensued trapping a good-for-nothing Yankee in the sacred precincts of the South. This northern transplant, Ignatius Ard, so named by a devout Greek Catholic mother, possessed one claim to fame—tempering the tones of a piano or guitar and using big words. An impressive vocabulary was of no benefit in cotton and tobacco fields or elsewhere; therefore, Ignatius stayed aloof from his ignorant neighbors. He chose his expected daughter's name after the midwife predicted the sex of the unborn by the way it was lying in its mother's womb. Before his son arrived, Ignatius was found drowned in the Little Pee Dee under unusual circumstances with the river being only four feet deep during a season of drought. Undoubtedly, the neighbors said, Cousin Ignatius could neither swim nor tread water. Hence, Deborah surmised, the *us* for a boy never replaced the *a* for a girl. How Cousin Theophila had won the fair hand of Cousin Hester was another mystery until Mama whispered that Vernie had been born six months after the wedding and that as far as she could see, the woods colt bore no resemblance to Cousin Theophila.

Mama privately referred to Cousin Hester as an outlaw not an in-law; nevertheless, even Jacob Jernigan was aware of her comeliness but piously remarked "pretty is as pretty does" when men friends noted charms of that "sho good-looking piece of woman flesh."

Mount Tabor all agreed that Cousin Theophila was a cuckold. Little boys spied behind potato banks and between corn rows and told tales, whether true or false, at the goings-on when Cousin Theophila was away at the tobacco market or posted on a deer stand during hunting season. However, Cousin Hester had not been caught in flagrante delicto and, furthermore, attended church every Sunday with her husband and Vernie, who was always dolled up in frilly clothes and feeling just as superior as she had demonstrated on that morning on the bus when Deborah had been dubbed Knee-deep-in-stockings. Cousin Hester, regardless of her extracurricular activities, was a good neighbor. Her warm broth was famous for settling stomach upsets, and she was the first to appear with a plate of fried chicken at the door of one who had "passed." Deborah remembered her soothing hands as she gave alcohol baths to bring down fever. Mama said, "Be what she may, Hester is a born nurse." Social exchanges, however, were limited to sickrooms, deathbeds and funerals, and occasional dinners on the ground at church. If Cousin Hester were aware of this line of demarcation, she did not say. Cousin Theophila, a man who preferred to keep to himself, did not seem to mind his family's exclusion. Tongues tittered behind his back about his inability "to get a woman with child," but when no future baby appeared, Mount Tabor women, some destined to produce annually, would have been happy to be privy to Cousin Hester's secret.

Deborah Jernigan found the Ards the most exciting family in Mount Tabor. Although she had no time for the snobby, over-dressed Vernie, she would often slip down the road to visit with Cousin Hester. The Ards lived in an unpainted wood frame shotgun house perched close to the side of the road. One could sit on the front porch and spit in the middle of the pavement if you were a good spitter like Aunt Martha. In the narrow strip between the house and the road was Cousin Hester's garden. Blue hydrangeas hugged the porch standing on cement blocks, and a trim row of boxwoods lined the short brick walk. In summer on either side grew a mass of zinnias, verbena, marigolds, dahlias, and four o'clocks. Cousin Hester laid out beds in geometric patterns of red, purple, white, and gold, and tended them as lovingly as she did a sick child. On one side close to the road stood a massive japonica which spread its wine-red roses in early fall to admiring eyes. It was Hester's pride and joy, it being the only one in Mount Tabor. On the opposite side a weeping willow flung her green tresses to the ground. When the road was widened after the Ards were no longer there, the house and garden disappeared under concrete over which drivers zipping by at sixty miles an hour took no thought of what once had been a miniature Eden. Deborah always slowed when she neared the site to remember long afternoons when she had sat with Cousin Hester, who loved to hear her stories and whose hands would pause over a dishpan of peas as she lost herself in a rendition of mythical heroes and romantic novels. Her deep brown eyes would stare vacantly across the road perhaps to an imaginary Mt. Olympus or Thornfield Hall, never seeing the long-leafed pines that dappled long shadows at sunset. There would be little conversation; only Deborah's animated voice as she opened doors to castles or painted pictures with some bits of poetry like "Old Phoebus rising from the sea" or recreated the melancholy roar that Sophocles heard on the Aegean.

Cousin Hester would murmur, "I wish Vernie liked books. I could have been a teacher, but my folks were too poor to send me to school. You know, I named Vernie, Vernal. I like green, don't you?" Deborah would nod her head solemnly and study the woman before her. The first thing you saw were the eyes—almost the color of black walnuts but flecked with gold. They seemed bottomless and although gently curved lips would sometimes smile, there was never a hint of laughter in her eyes. Seldom did she look at Deborah squarely and even then her gaze would soon return to the busyness of her hands or stray to a distant sprig of verbena or a butterfly hovering in search of nectar. A mass of rich brown hair belonged to the small shapely head. She wore it pulled back loosely from a high forehead from which a few tendrils escaped. Hairpins anchored a large bun at the nape of her neck. Her voice Deborah loved. Like the Shakespearean description, it was "ever low and sweet" with the words flowing adagio. The only trouble was that she spoke so infrequently, but Deborah suspected that plaintive arias lay unheard—buried scales Cousin Hester was afraid to vocalize. Gradually, Deborah developed a deep affection, born first out of curiosity and later into something that she could not name—closeness like sisters but not exactly sisters. Cousin Hester was somewhere out there; Deborah was here but sensed a common ground if only Cousin Hester would share it.

One afternoon when Mama and Daddy had left Deborah to tend store while they went to Florence "to buy Santa Claus" for seven children and eight grandchildren, Deborah, having had no customers for hours, locked the doors to the country commissary and ambled down the road to Cousin Hester's. Mama had noted the frequency of her daughter's visits to what she called "the woman of ill repute" and had voiced strong objections. Deborah's quick retort was that this so-called Delilah was quite welcome when an extra hand was needed in the sickroom or in the kitchen during the canning season. The time seemed propitious to call, for she had heard that Vernie was visiting a cousin over the river, and Cousin Theophila had been seen earlier meandering down the road with mule and wagon, his destination the savannah to gather firewood. As Deborah approached the yard, she noted that Emily Dickinson's "blond assassin" had visited the little garden, the only color being a lone japonica arrayed in bluish pink buds swollen with the promise of bloom. Knocking on the door, she could hear the faint exchange of voices, followed by the back door closing. At the same time she spotted Fred Small's red Ford parked in the churchyard diagonal from the house. Fred was a Clemson man and had been teaching agriculture and shop in the high school for as long as Deborah could remember. Rumor had it that he might be queer. Not bad looking and a nice enough fellow in his forties, he lived alone in a brick house with no sign of marrying and starting a family like decent men should. The would-be visitor smiled to herself as she waited, deciding that she had stumbled on something that would be of interest to Mount Tabor. It seemed an inopportune time to call, but just as she was about to abandon the visit, Cousin Hester opened the door and beckoned her in. Cousin Hester wore a loose yellow housedress splashed with garnet roses. There was nothing unkempt about her appearance except for the bun that appeared slightly awry, suggesting that the hairpins had not secured it.

"Come in, Deborah," she said softly. "I was just getting ready to sample the fruit cake. It just came out of the oven. Would you like a taste?"

Deborah followed her through the neat rooms that marched to the kitchen. It was surprisingly pleasant to Deborah, who had not seen it before. The square table in the middle of the room was laid with a red-checked oil cloth that matched the ruffled country curtains over the single window. On the eyes of the woodstove sat a set of pots in red enamel flecked in white. Near the stove was a sink with a red pump, a luxury for the women in Mount Tabor, most of whom drew dishwater from the well that stood in every yard. On a rack close to the pie safe, an upright wooden cabinet, was a triple row of hooks from which dangled brightly colored cups. The smell of cinnamon and cloves suffused the tiny room and soon the guest found herself drinking coffee laced with thick cream from a green cup and nibbling on a slice of black cake rich with nuts and fruit. As they sat on benches opposite each other, Deborah felt the awkwardness of the situation and found herself without words. There were several moments of silence. At last her hostess looked straight into her eyes.

"Mr. Small is my friend," she said. "He bought me them pots and give me that pump. He is real nice to me. He says I could have been a real good Home Ec teacher. I wouldn't a wanted to do that. I spend most of my time with house things. Gets old after a time. I would have liked to tell stories like you and maybe write down some of my own. I love to hear about them gods and goddesses and them romance stories like when Jane finds Mr. Rochester." She dropped her eyes to the coffee which she took straight and which matched the color of her eyes. She took a sip and once again turned her gaze to her guest.

"Sometime words come to me and I see things I almost forgot. I wish I could write them down, but they'd sound crazy to anybody 'cept me. And there ain't much time what with the house and garden and the fieldwork. Still," she paused and peered into the dregs of her cup as if to situate a memory.

"What kinds of things, Cousin Hester?"

"Like the way owls screech and come close to the house before somebody dies. Two of em set up a squall right outside my window in the peach tree the night granny passed. Or the way the grass feels under your feet when you first go barefoot in May. Or how the sun creeps up out of the gray ocean and turns the water into sparkles. Or like the first taste of fruitcake when it's soft with homemade blackberry wine after it's been a whole year since Christmas," she finished. She smiled as she fingered a crumb and tasted it. "I wish I knew how to put smells and tastes in words."

"You just did," Deborah said softly. "Cousin Hester, why doesn't Mr. Small take you away from here? I don't mean to his house at Union Grove. I mean far away."

"He would, but there's Vernie. Theophila is no Daddy to her. I'm not much of a mother either," she added.

"Vernie can take care of herself. You know she's not smart in books. She's always repeating a grade. She's going to be married to some plow hand as soon as she can find one."

"I know," she whispered. "I want a better life for Vernal. Seems like we never could get along. Not even when she was a baby." With her empty coffee cup she traced the squares on the tablecloth. Her cake lay half eaten. Deborah had also lost her taste for cake. Her throat tightened and she dropped her eyes to conceal the tears she was afraid would come.

At that moment the back door opened and Cousin Theophila entered with arms ladened with stove wood. He did not acknowledge Deborah's presence. Instead, he whiffed the air and whined with the voice of a termagant. "Why ain't you got my supper on the table? Some days you ain't worth a pinch of chicken shit." Cousin Hester's hand trembled as she quietly replaced her cup in the saucer.

Seconds later, Deborah, with murder in her heart, found herself in the backyard and running toward the store. There were two cars, a stripped down Ford and a pickup waiting. Big Joe already had the pump nozzle in his tank and was sitting on his horn to alert the owner of the closed store. Bubba Williams was also waiting. In the absence of a newspaper, Bubba was the clarion for Mount Tabor. Most folks called him "news toter." Clad in a dirty undershirt and faded dungarees, he stood rolling Prince Albert tobacco between a sheet of thin white paper. With a quick lick of his tongue, he sealed the cigarette, thrust it between his lips, and then groped in his pocket for a match. Unsuccessful, he approached Big Joe who had just clicked the nozzle to complete his five-dollar purchase.

"Gimme a light, Joe."

Big Joe tossed a box of Quick Light matches to Bubba with a "Keep 'em."

As Bubba cupped his hands to light, he said to no one in particular, "Reckon you ain't heard the latest. Vernie Ard is done run off with Dick Martin. He's three times her age. Robbing the cradle. Reckon like Mama, like daughter, eh?" he chuckled.

"I wouldn't know, Bubba. Maybe you been dipping in the pot yourself and know firsthand."

"Not me. I ain't messing with Theophila Ard dumb as he is." Big Joe handed Deborah a crumpled bill and shuffled off to the open door of his pickup.

"You ain't heard from Rupert, Joe?" Bubba asked. The answer was lost in the churn of the motor as Big Joe lurched off toward the road.

Bubba, who had not the slightest fear of blowing himself up to kingdom come, puffed on his cigarette as he eyed the gas gauge fall to two gallons. Following Deborah into the store, he fished out coins from one pocket then the other, counting out ten pennies to complete the purchase.

"Bubba, where did you hear about Vernie? Is Dick going to marry her? She's not old enough to marry. Her parents would have to sign to give consent."

"Reckon they won't have no choice after them running off together. Reckon Theophila will be glad to put his John Henry on any paper. Anyhow, reckon Dick needed a woman pretty bad to take care of his two younguns. She ain't much older than they is. And his wife, Della, ain't been dead even a year."

Deborah tried desperately to conjure up a picture of Vernie in the maternal role, but as prolific as her imagination was, nothing emerged. What was very real to her was Cousin Hester's soft voice, "But there's Vernie."

When school opened after New Year's Day, the boys in the

shop were sent to study hall. Their teacher, Mr. Small, had resigned during the holidays. On New Year's Eve, while Theophila was killing a six-point buck before deer season closed January 1, Cousin Hester also closed the door to the house that had been her home for thirteen odd years. Deborah could imagine her plucking a japonica from the bush of which she was so proud and perhaps sticking it in a buttonhole of her coat. No one in Mount Tabor witnessed her departure, and no one ever saw or heard from her again. Mr. Small was rapidly replaced by a local farmer who knew, according to the school board, more about growing corn and building whatnots and babies' high chairs than most of them college men. Years later, while Deborah was leafing through the magazine *Poetry*, she found these lines:

> Phoebus climbed over the vernal line of the Aegean,
> Shook out a bagful of sunbeams
> And left them shimmering on Neptune's undulating breast.
> —Anonymous

The State Highway Department adopted the road through Mount Tabor, widening it to serve as a short cut to the beach. Even so, in the spring purple verbena and an occasional clump of daffodils sprang through the gravel of the macadam shoulders.

CHAPTER

Thirteen

PROM NIGHT

There was rightness in labeling certain regions Bible Belt. It girded the Low Country of South Carolina, buckling tight its people. Its sprocket hooked the sinner and the saint, the innocent and the guilty, the lowly and the high. On its strap hung an invisible pager—a device not to be seen in reality until years later, but its tongue commanded the inhabitants of Mount Tabor with its "Thou shalt nots." To disobey its call was anathema; to unbuckle the safety belt landed the miscreant in a burning ring of fire, where the flames were never quenched and where the proverbial rich man who refused Lazarus the crumbs from his scrumptious table begged eternally for a drop of water to ease his parching tongue. Jacob Jernigan and many like him felt no constraints in its hold. Rather it gave him the support he needed for the vicissitudes of daily life and the security of a safe landing.

95

To others, however, its grip bound them to a black and white world—where red on lips and nails personified Jezebel, who was fed to the dogs. Her color winked at the imbiber of sparkling burgundy, brew which Mount Tabor had not tasted even vicariously.

On a Sunday afternoon in late May, seventeen-year-old Deborah sat on the front steps playing with that other world as vivid to her as the blue hydrangeas which sprawled along the base of the house. As she eyed the pink thrift creeping effortlessly along the concrete walkway and poppies scattered in wild profusion on either side, she smiled. Nature had sloughed restriction right under the nose of Mount Tabor. Passersby stopped their cars to admire Anna Jernigan's poppies, their scarlet petals opening seductively to reveal purple throats, a sensual invitation to hummingbirds and bees. Nobody guessed this collage in scarlet, sisters of a more potent species, was capable of producing euphoria more powerful than wine, an anodyne sought for centuries by saint, sinner, aesthete, scholar. Deborah had heard that quite a few Confederate matrons had found respite in its pod, transforming the finality of death to bittersweet memories and dulling the fear of that SOB Sherman. Now Deborah, like Keats, yearned for some opiate to lift her out of the doldrums. She wondered if Mama would miss the homemade brew, fermented nectar from the grape arbors, sealed in fruit jars secreted behind two rows of tomatoes on the top shelf in the smokehouse. Everybody except Mama knew that the wine was made only for sousing Christmas fruitcake. Only she could use it to settle her "bad stomach," a condition concurrent with her pregnancy with Deborah. The malady still plagued her at times and explained her secret visits to the smokehouse. Poor Mama! Daddy said jokingly she had craved wine when she was in the family way like some women craved raw dough, but Deborah suspected that her thirst might be akin to her confederate grandmothers. Medicinal use gave it legitimacy even in the Bible Belt.

Tonight was Prom Night at Union Grove. No gown hung in

her closet and no corsage was expected to arrive with a young man in his Sunday suit. The junior class had pushed back the bleachers and transformed the gymnasium into a garden with an arched trellis of ivy interspersed with seasonal magnolias under which seniors and their dates would enter and be ushered by juniors to their tables. From a juke box borrowed from a local cafe strains of "Springtime in the Rockies" would float across the sports arena as couples took to the floor in a waltz or foxtrot. For the first time there would be dancing at the Junior-Senior Prom. Some brave soul had loosened the belt.

The spirited junior class sponsor, Miss Cole, fresh out of college, looked with horror at the spectacle of a prom devoid of music and dance, however florally decorated and attended by gowned young ladies with suited dates. Ignoring the strictness imposed by Bible Belt canon, Miss Cole had enriched the physical education curriculum with the waltz, venturing even further, as her Astaire-Rogers novices progressed into the jitterbug. Last she added Latin flavor with the rumba and tango. To protect the gym floor, the budding Terpsichoreans shed their shoes and danced recesses away. Even Knee-deep-in-stockings had found a partner in Julian, who lost some of his fear of girls with the equally shy Deborah. At first the two moved as mechanically as robots but gradually they limbered to the strings of Guy Lombardo or Tommy Dorsey. Of course, dancing was even more sinful than playing ball, because it added the physical temptation with the closeness of boy and girl. Julian's parents, non-churchgoers, had no objection to this matter. Deborah, who felt not even the first twinge of conscience, feared only that Daddy would find out that his daughter, touched at birth by the hand of God, had succumbed to worldly follies.

As Prom Night neared and the news of Miss Cole's foot-tapping class had not invaded the Jernigan household, Deborah had said yes to Julian's invitation. Certainly he was no knight in shining armor, but at least he was taller than she and his stammer would not matter on the dance floor. As a junior, Deborah had not gone to the prom. Nobody had asked her, but she didn't feel too bad, thinking the occasion a sticky affair with dinner served by the PTA and silly speeches poking fun at the outgoing seniors. This year was different. Her straight brown hair had been permanent waved and fell in a soft pageboy to her shoulders. Beryl had slipped her cosmetics, including a pink lipstick and a pencil to accent her eyebrows. Julian wouldn't care if in the car she put finishing touches on her face. Now the affair had taken on color. In a green evening dress that she had seen in Ringel's in Georgetown and matching satin slippers, she would show Union Grove that a scholar could turn siren and she would walk in beauty in the night just as Byron had described. When Knee-deep-in-stockings became the butt of a junior joke, she would smile charmingly and join in the clapping. Such was the beginning of her anticipation. She found herself embroidering her plans with fanciful dreams of turning gangly Julian into a handsome escort who bowed to her graciously at the end of the final dance and who kissed her goodnight at the door. The red roses that had encircled her wrist would be pressed between the leaves of a scrapbook newly purchased to record the beginning of a new life where the colors of the rainbow streaked across the darkness of that other world. She had murmured at midnight in the silence of her room, "We are such stuff as dreams are made on." Now as she sat on the step on Prom Night, another quotation was on her lips: "Oh, what fools we mortals be!"

Mother's Day had been two weeks ago. It was the same annual occasion when children and grandchildren gathered to pay homage to motherhood. Anna Jernigan had been pleased with her sundry gifts—a lamp made of seashells (tacky, Deborah thought); handmade aprons, lavishly embroidered with loving sentiments; an artificial corsage; a teaspoon bearing the name *Miami Beach*, proof of a recent visit. Beryl, however had brought a three-tiered white enamel planter capable of holding Mama's asparagus ferns and angel-wing begonias. Beryl's successful husband, Robert, knowing Anna's secret visits to the smokehouse, gave her a bottle of brandy he had acquired at the airport, a lagniappe from one of his business excursions. Anna's face had turned scarlet. A low chuckle ran through the family as Robert hastily remarked, "It's for fruitcake, Miss Anna." Recovering quickly, she thanked him, but the winks and smiles had not escaped her. The cat was out of the bag. So French cognac took its place behind the tomatoes—proof to everyone that Anna knew its purpose. Gamin, however, could not suppress his giggles, thoroughly enjoying his mother's embarrassment. Perhaps he was remembering being required to drop basketball, it being the devil's game with young people running around half-naked and people betting on the outcome. Lily, the sister who had just obtained license to preach in the Church of God in her community, had patted her Mama on the back and said jokingly, "We not looking for another little sister, are we? I hear the one we have has joined her classmates and learned to dance. Sister Thomas tells me you can hear a gramophone going nonstop at Union Grove. Gonna have dancing at the Junior-Senior this year."

All eyes turned on Deborah except Beryl, who shot Lily an angry message. "What's wrong with dancing? Robert and I are taking lessons at Arthur Murray's now. Once a month friends of ours go out to dinner and dancing. I can't imagine that there wasn't dancing at the marriage of Cana when Jesus turned the water into wine." Deborah looked at her sister gratefully.

Jacob Jernigan abruptly changed the subject. "Well, Mama, what's in that big box that you haven't opened?" His gift to her was an electric mixer. Deborah, however, knew that the subject was not closed.

"Daughter, I want to have a word with you." This had come after a late supper as the three had finished leftovers. Deborah followed him to the porch. He sat down in one of the wooden rockers, pulling another one near to him and motioning her to sit down. He clasped his big hands under his chin in the attitude of prayer. His eyes studied distance as he waited.

"Yes, Daddy, I have learned to dance and Julian has invited

me to the Junior-Senior Prom. Julian is my friend. I can't see any harm in learning to dance. Besides, it's good exercise."

The air was so still. Not a leaf moved. A navy blue cloud behind the barn had eclipsed a rosy sunset. A jagged streak of lightning knifed the dark cloud, followed by a low rumble of thunder, the harbinger of rain.

"Looks like a cloud is coming up. It will be good for the crops," Deborah commented.

"Yes," he said, "we had special prayers for rain tonight in church. Some folks had to plant corn three times and still can't get a stand. Rain's not the only thing we prayed for DE-Borah." He pronounced it the old way.

Anger washed over her as powerful as the storm now heralding its approach with deep-throated thunder. For the moment, the loving father vanished; the creature sitting beside her was a stranger. Never had his strong hands punished her. Now she wanted violence that would alienate him even more. Her next words shook him.

"Take off your belt, Jacob Jernigan, and give me a good strapping. I am quite ready to pay for my sins. Be sure to draw blood. What are the words? 'By his stripes we are healed.' Play God. Punish me. I won't even shed a tear. You know what you have done to me? You have turned what should be a loving God into a nemesis, who pours out his wrath on helpless children. I'm sick of him."

His hand clutched his heart as his head dropped on the arm of the wooden chair. "Blasphemy!" he choked. An awful sound came from his throat just as a peal of thunder shook the house.

"Mama!" Deborah screamed.

His first heart attack at sixty-five. For two weeks he had been lying in the hospital. The doctors said he needed rest. She had not gone to visit him. All the others had gathered around his bed. Only she and he knew what had transpired, though he had not said a single word. Every day he had asked for her. Today she had sent him a note. "I'm not going to the prom. Get well soon. I love

100

you. Deborah"

Tomorrow he would be coming home. She knew he would never mention her terrible words, and there would be a silence, palpable as the stone heavy in her chest. It had closed the door between them. Begging forgiveness was admitting contrition. She remembered the Centurion's prayer: "Speak the word only." But she couldn't find the word. Neither Deborah Jernigan nor Knee-deep-in-stockings could say "Father, forgive me," which would make him rejoice that his beloved daughter had seen the light. "I should have been named Dinah," she mused. Defiance of her father, old Jacob of the Bible, had brought only brief happiness before death. She looked down at forbidden shorts she was wearing—sawed off pants. Mama hadn't noticed when she left for the hospital with Gamin. Wiping tears on the unhemmed legs, she did not notice Julian approach.

"Deborah, how's your dad?" In blue overalls with hands in his pockets, he had little resemblance to the young Lochinvar of the West. Still his voice was soft. She suspected that he knew the truth—that reneging on his invitation had a deeper reason than the one she had given, the illness of her father. He, too, would not be at the prom.

Instead of answering his question, she asked, "Julian, have you ever had a drink?" Her startling words completely obliterated his stammer.

"Why, no, Deb. Can't say I have except, you know, wine at Christmas time. Why?"

"I mean a real one. Like French cognac."

"No, I can't say I have."

"Then let's have one. Our own celebration."

"I don't know. Your folks."

"Safe for at least three hours."

On the far end of the porch curtained by wisteria climbing the trellis, Deborah poured the amber liquid into a clear glass custard cup, a reasonable substitute for a brandy snifter. She handed it to Julian and then poured one for herself.

"Let's do it proper," she said, as she twirled the glass slowly. "We join the elite band of brandy snifters. She touched her glass to his. "To the prom, Julian." Their eyes met as they raised their drinks.

The first sips—a strange sweetness with a tingle and a warmth running down a golden path inside—suffused their cheeks with color.

"No wonder Mama has been sampling," she giggled. "She's going to think some thief broke into the smokehouse and stole her booze. Poor Mama!"

"Poor Mama," Julian parroted and joined her laughter.

"Maybe Mama and I got more in common than I thought," she mused soberly.

The world was beginning to look very different. This magical liquid, wand of Bacchus, was waving over a friendlier world, a world aglow like the sunset limning a purple cloud hanging low in the west. "No wonder the Greeks thought there was a god in wine," she laughed. Later, as they drained the last drops, Deborah extended her empty glass that didn't quite make contact with her partner's. "To Daddy," she whispered. Picking up the empty bottle, she hung it tenderly in the wisteria and draped it in a blue cluster, heavy with scent.

As she turned toward Julian, he was surprised to see tears running down her cheeks. He reached out his arms to her and said with unfeigned gallantry without a trace of a stammer, "May I have this dance, Miss Jernigan?"

Years later, Deborah would wish that the lens of a video camera could have preserved the figures of two misfits, a boy in overalls and a girl in sawed off pants, humming "Moonlight and Roses" as they waltzed along the porch occasionally bumping into rockers. Only the birds flitting homeward heard the duet, but an early evening star winked at their mischief as a full moon smiled down approvingly.

CHAPTER

Fourteen

DARKNESS AT NOON

I t was the day of the eclipse. The clock on the mantel in the parlor had just struck noon—twelve chimes that Deborah through the years had associated with birth or death, the precise interpretation dependent upon the mood which sometimes vacillated like the pendulum of the ancient timepiece, its face yellowed and stained with water drops the night an unnamed hurricane flew in from the Atlantic. Though it splintered the right wing of the guardian angel on the mahogany case, the old horologe defied the wind that slashed the two-hundred-year-old oak and remained ticking even as it leaned precariously, like a Tower of Pisa, on the marble bust of Beethoven, great-grandmother's prize in the piano competition at the Seminary for Young Ladies in Charleston. Of course, her attendance was before "the war," when the Jernigan landholdings cut a broad swath of bottom land bounding the Great Pee Dee River, now gone with the wind like the wing of the mutilated angel. But the clock endured like Faulkner's Dilsey. Such was the first miracle ascribed to the mighty hand of God that dictated the movement of the clock especially on auspicious occasions like that morning when it struck midnight proclaiming Deborah Jernigan's birth. The father had said it was a miracle, but on the field of a child's vision mischievous shades of light and dark played, creating the tapestry of that morning. The darkness of the midnight hour, the bleat of the newborn infant, and the wail of the reluctant mother—all seemed incongruent poetically with a miracle more appropriate to sunrise with both mother and daughter making joyful noises to the Lord. "Blasphemy" would she whisper as she smiled. How dare Jacob's daughter question the power of the Almighty! But question she did as she fingered the notes of Tchaikovsky's "Dance of the Dying Doll" on the enameled keys of the upright piano, yellowed like the face of the clock and chipped like the angel. Would it not be a miracle if, within a few minutes, it struck thirteen times as it was reported to have done the night that Sherman razed the state capitol? At six minutes past the hour, the moon would cast her shadow between the earth and sun, dropping premature darkness. Most of the inhabitants of Mount Tabor were unaware of celestial movement. At this time of year their orbit encompassed the fields of tobacco, where croppers were even now stripping ripe leaves from the stalks—green gold hauled in mule-drawn drays to the barn sheds where the process would begin to string gummy bunches of the weed to sticks to be hung in the barn and slowly cooked by gas or wood furnaces until the green had disappeared and only the gold remained. Each broad leaf would once again be transferred to green, this time bills, the number determining whether the fertilizer could be paid in full with enough left over for trading perhaps a five-year-old car or purchasing another farm as was Jacob Jernigan's wont as he envisioned the fulfillment of a dream, leaving each of his seven children a home. Not so with his daughter. Green gold meant neither land nor cars but a ticket to college and escape from Mount Tabor, where love lived side by side with guilt and despair. Since her Daddy's heart attack, light seldom penetrated the darkness of Deborah Jernigan's horizon. Her Mother and Daddy knew she had made applications to college and had been accepted. Neither had discussed it with her although she had heard the arguments between them late at night or early in the morning when they thought she was asleep. Anna Jernigan saw no reason why a high school diploma shouldn't be enough. It had been adequate for the others. Besides, the two years of typing, bookkeeping, and shorthand would enable her to get a job in a local lawyer's office. And besides, Deborah had never been strong, and going off to a strange place away from a mother's watchful eye might bring on another bout with pneumonia. Anyway, they needed the money to add to their savings account; that is, if the tobacco brought a good price. Jacob Jernigan had mumbled half-hearted agreement with his wife. Through the years, he had usually acquiesced to her demands. In her heart Deborah knew that his reasons for not sending her away to school did not coincide with those of his wife. Education and godless teachers might drive her even farther from salvation, and she would be lost for him here on earth as well as for all eternity. Oddly enough, Deborah felt his sorrow keenly. Anger had gradually dissipated, but the hurt remained. She missed the clasp of his strong hands and the pride in his eyes when she excelled in school. Because of his illness, he had not gone to her high school graduation and, therefore, had not heard the tribute she had made to him in her valedictory address. Nevertheless, she had put a copy of her speech in his Bible where undoubtedly her message had been eclipsed by her allusions to philosophers and poets. All he had said was "You're a smart girl, Deborah," but his voice lacked the usual warmth.

Now as she sat turning a trill into a dirge, she waited for a miracle emanating not from a clock, but from any source that would influence her father's decision to grant her wish. At that moment the lace curtains filtering the August sun turned to a dusty gray as the cabbage roses in the wool rug lost their pinkness. From the chicken yard came the sound of a rooster crowing. Darkness at midday was falling upon Mount Tabor. Undoubtedly astonished field workers would fall between rows of tobacco and wait for the end of time.

She noticed first his feet encased in his house slippers. Jacob Jernigan stood in the doorway, a twilight figure holding his Bible in one hand and his gold-rimmed glasses in the other. It was as though he had shed his spectacles to test his vision. Somewhere the brakes on a car squealed, and at that moment she realized that the clock had stopped ticking. In a flash she knew two things: first, last night she had forgotten to wind the clock; second, that Jacob Jernigan had heard nothing about the lunar eclipse. She knew also that the man in the doorway who believed that the sun had stood still at the command of Joshua and that the shape of the earth was four-cornered because the Holy Bible said so, would take these two incidents as a direct message from the celestial throne. The question was, how would he interpret these two events? Should she confess her negligence in winding the clock and then explain the sudden darkness? In truth, time seemed suspended as she struggled to make a decision that might determine the course of her life.

"Daddy," she whispered. Her eyes locked his. "It's all right," she added. She would unveil the mystery.

"It's all right, daughter." This was the term he used when he was most serious. It was the appellation he used when he explained the pride he took in new ground cleared for his children or the solace he had given her after she had thrust into the fire the doll gowned in a replica of her mother's wedding dress, the gift from Santa Claus, instead of the wished-for bicycle. "God has spoken," he continued. "I'm going to find the money to send you to college. Just don't ever get beyond your raisings," he added.

At that moment the moon's shadow moved from the face of the sun as light twinkled through the curtains casting harmless spots on the now pink rug. The clock, however, did not resume its counting of the hours. Jacob Jernigan did not notice. He held his daughter in his arms, his unshaved cheek pressed against hers.

"Thank you, Daddy," she sobbed brokenly. "Forgive me," she whispered.

His response took her by surprise. "Do you believe in miracles now?"

"Yes! Oh, yes!" she whispered. He would never guess the searing guilt that riddled her words.

CHAPTER

Fifteen

THE QUILT

For as long as she could remember she had waited for this day. At the foot of her bed lay the locker trunk securely fastened, its brass key on a brand new chain supporting also the letter J. She might have chosen D for Deborah, the name to which she had answered for seventeen years. The preference had been deliberate. She was abandoning the old identity and taking on a new one. Now on that last morning, at sunrise—before Daddy rose to cook the grits, fry the bacon, scramble the eggs—she pondered the Deborah days. The light filtering through the organdy curtains dappled the quilt she had pulled up on this mid-September morning, chilly for this time of year.

Mama had made this quilt especially for her "baby," a name anathema for one asserting independence. The squares on the counterpane, a collage of past dresses, bore witness to her life in Mount Tabor. All the Easter dresses and birthday frocks were there, miniature scraps preserved from outgrown clothes and cut just so to fill the sewing basket.

One winter evening, Anna Jernigan, as was her wont, sat by the fireside laying squares on a homespun rectangle, moving them like checkers to effect a harmonious array. She held up a bright scrap of yellow shantung and asked, "Baby, remember this dress? You were five years old. I bought it at Ringel's in Georgetown. It was on sale, but Mrs. Ringel cut it down to four-ninety-eight. I thought it was a steal for that price. Remember it had a big sash and pockets appliquéd with lilies. So appropriate for Easter. My baby was the best-dressed little girl in church with white slippers and matching yellow socks and a big yellow bow in her hair."

"I remember, Mama." The words were meant for a dismissal, not a stirring up of remembrances of things past. Besides, yellow was the color she hated most.

Anna chuckled as she held up a bit of velvet—a deep burgundy. "Oh, my! You remember the little red coat? It had gray fur around the collar and pockets. Where the double stitching ended in points, there were little blue flowers. When you saw that coat, you wouldn't even look at another. You called it a princess coat. Got the idea, I reckon, from one of them books you always had in your hands. Anyway, when I said it was too expensive, you jumped up and down and said if you couldn't have that one, you wouldn't have any." She paused and stared vacantly into the past. "That was the year it rained all summer. The corn shriveled up and died in the field. One night an old hen and her biddies drowned. We had a hard time paying the fertilizer bill. You remember, Jacob," she interposed. "But I wanted my baby to have the best. You looked just like a doll in it. Remember, baby?"

"Mama, my name is Deborah. I am your last-born, but I am not a baby. I no longer play with dolls, nor did I ever look like one." Deborah turned to her book, avoiding the tears that she imagined were welling in her mother's eyes.

"Slip of the tongue, Deborah," she apologized. "I should remember you outgrew dolls years ago."

At that moment mother and daughter looked into the glowing embers of the log fire; both saw the flames curl around a princess doll in a flowing white organdy dress.

Jacob Jernigan dropped his Bible to his knees and peered over his gold-rimmed glasses to assess the situation. First, he looked at his daughter; then at his wife. He stood ready to curb a crisis with his "Tut, tut." Deborah caught the no-no nod of his head, though Anna's gaze had returned to the velvet square that she placed next to the blue wool jumper. Jacob was grateful for the silence that ensued and once again picked up his Bible and returned to Holy Writ.

Now as she lay under the completed quilt, she thought of Frost's "Death of the Hired Man": I know just how it is to find the right words to say too late.

The quilt had been a graduation gift. Deborah had not seen the laborious whipping out of a sack of last year's cotton crop converted to a smooth sheet now encased between bright squares and a green satin lining. Green was her favorite color. Nor had she been present when Mount Tabor ladies met for a quilting bee to vie with each other for Mistress of Stitch Craft. Rotund Aunt Fanny was usually the winner. She had only one good eye; the other lost to her cow Bossy's kick and replaced with blue glass that stared like an angel in a graveyard was an ill match to her brown seeing eye. Aunt Fanny's nimble fat fingers could whip uniform stitches in any design—circles, squares, triangles. She was the fastest lady sitting around the frame suspended from the ceiling and supporting the new quilt. Even her occasional visit to the snuff can did not slow her down.

The finished product has been secretly tucked away until graduation night. Daddy's gift had been a pasteboard card large enough to accommodate the eleven silver dollars taped in a circle. In his free flowing cursive he had written in the circle: *One for each year. Congratulations. Love, Daddy.* The Bible verse that usually accompanied his gifts was not there, its absence a token of the estrangement that followed that Sunday afternoon when he had uttered the terrible word BLASPHEMY. Mama's gift was in a white cardboard box, the one which had housed the chenille bedspread ordered from Sears Roebuck. In the center was a corsage of lacy green asparagus fern snipped from the cement urns flanking the front steps on the porch. Three red rosebuds shorn of their thorns completed the arrangement. There was no note. Deborah, however, had draped it over her white graduation dress and had paraded around saying, "Call me Joseph. I wear a coat of many colors." Everyone had laughed at the new graduate's chicanery. Now she remembered that she had not said, "Thank you."

Since the day of the eclipse when Jacob Jernigan had interpreted the darkness at noon as a message from on high, his daughter had counted the days. Since that day Anna Jernigan had cried—not constantly, but when any mention of assembling a wardrobe or purchasing luggage was made, her voice would tremble at the edges and her apron would brush her eyes. Deborah pretended not to notice either the tears or the aloofness of her father. She marked off the days on the calendar each night. At times bitterness that she could taste in her mouth welled up. Why couldn't she have parents like other girls? Why couldn't they be proud of their child who would be the first to enter the halls of Minerva? Open rebellion accompanied this bitterness. She painted her fingernails, rouged her cheeks, penciled her eyebrows, and splashed her lips in ruby red to display a smile larger than that of Joan Crawford. Actually it was more of a smirk than a smile. No reprimand followed. She pondered the change in them. She supposed they had given up on her. They had relegated her to the devil. Their indifference, however, had tempered the ebullience she might have had. They had no right, she thought. It wasn't fair.

One day as she sat at the sewing machine making the red-checked bedspreads for twin beds in her college room, Anna Jernigan had asked, "Deborah, will you be taking the quilt with you? It would come in handy on a cold night."

"Oh, no, Mama. A blanket will be enough. You know the

dorms are centrally heated. Besides, it wouldn't go with these spreads."

"I just thought," she offered timidly, "you could bring it out on a cold night. You know how easy it is for you to catch colds. You have already had . . ."

"Pneumonia three times," she cut in. "Well, maybe I'll have it a fourth time. Rather that than be a country bumpkin dragging a homemade quilt to school." Her words hissed like vipers that struck Anna Jernigan, whose hands covered her face as if to ward off another attack. She made a hasty exit to the kitchen.

Two angers boiled inside Deborah—anger at her mother but also anger at herself. There would be no joy in leave taking. There would only be guilt as sharp as her waspish words. To be herself, to assert her being, she had alienated the two people who had watched over her sick bed, loved her despite her mean spirited-ness, and sacrificed their pitiful savings.

Now on this last morning in the room where she had charted her course, her little craft lacked stability. Waves of guilt lashed her even as she knew there was no turning back. Suppose the christening of her new identity swept her into waters too deep for swimming. Suppose her meager country education was not sturdy enough to battle the open seas of higher learning, and she would be ferried home to face Mount Tabor ridicule. Of course, she would be welcomed with open arms by her father, because God had punished her pride with defeat and brought low one who had violated the Fifth Commandment, "Honor thy father and thy mother."

She heard Daddy sharpen the knife on the whetstone in preparation for slicing the ham, a treat reserved for special occasions. Soon it would be sizzling in the black cast iron frying pan. Then she heard the squeak of the door to her parents' bedroom. Mama was getting up and going to the kitchen, an unusual event unless there was company in the house. Otherwise, she would wait for Daddy to bring her morning coffee. Yes, there was someone extra this morning, a stranger among them.

Deborah slipped the quilt from her bed and made a robe for herself, lifting the excess with her arms and framing her face like a newborn's hooded blanket. Now she stood in the kitchen door.

"Jacob," Anna said, "I got up to fix the eggs. You know how she likes them. Sunny side up but not the white runny. You always get them too hard or too soft."

"I know, Anna. Our baby's gonna leave us. You mustn't cry today. It will make her feel bad. We got to bear up."

"I know, Jacob. And let me make the redeye gravy. Thin grits and gravy with eggs was about the only thing she would eat when she was coming out of a spell of sickness."

It was somebody else's turn to cry. Deborah's voice quivered. "Daddy," she said, a shade too brightly, "Do you suppose we can get this quilt in the trunk? Your baby might need it. I hear it snows often in Columbia."

A smile wreathed Anna Jernigan's face. It had moved slowly from her wide lips up to her eyes where it sparkled and lit her small frame. She held three eggs in her hand. "Sunnyside up?" she questioned.

"Sunnyside up," was the quick response.

CHAPTER

Sixteen

IN THE HALLS OF MINERVA

Centering the circular driveway that sliced a wide expanse of grass and trees stood a stone pedestal. It supported an oval bowl from which a fine mist sprayed. Amid this watery isle rose Pallas Athena, the sculptured goddess of wisdom, peering at incoming quaking freshmen with owlish eyes on registration day. Only the olive branch that she extended from her right arm softened the austerity of her gaze. Behind her stood her temple cast in ageing brick fronted with massive white Ionic columns. A bell tower topped the third story of this center edifice. Wild tales had it that each Halloween at midnight, a shrouded figure in black stole into the tower to ring the bell thirteen times, commemorating the tragedy of a heartbroken lass who had jumped to her death the night her soldier sweetheart was felled by one of Sherman's bullets. To add to the lore, the more imaginative speculated that the owl-eyed goddess, enemy of Mars, had

114

protected the campus, even though that devil had razed Columbia. Whether or not her aegis, historically a shield upon which the Medusa coiled and hissed, had spared one of the oldest women's colleges in the South, there it stood—almost a hundred years old. The main building housed administration and classrooms. Like a mother hen it spread its wings to protect the dormitories on either side. Once again Athene surveyed a new class file into the halls of learning. Four years later, she would also watch a gaggle of out-going seniors, spirited on the wings of Bacchus to the watery isle, lifting their white graduation skirts to pay homage. Deborah Jernigan, among them, would swear that the frozen lips of the goddess were smiling at their caprices even as her owlish eyes twinkled. But that scene, as Marlowe avowed, would be "in another country" and while "the wench" would not be dead, great changes would have taken place.

Today, however, Deborah, standing in her brown and white saddle oxfords five feet six and weighing in at eighty-nine pounds, would follow docilely from registrar to business office to dormitory. Fully aware that her skirt and blouse bore the label Sears Roebuck, she smiled and nodded at her new classmates and found herself at intervals clutching her father's hand. Inept at small talk, she wondered if the curriculum offered a course to girls fresh from the farm, who, though book literate, were ignorant socially and inexperienced. At eighteen, she had never had a date and had been kissed twice, once by Rupert, perhaps lying in an unmarked grave in North Africa, and once by stammering Julius as they danced on her front porch on prom night. Suddenly she saw her mother, tears burning behind her eyes, as she slipped in her hand a ten-dollar bill through the car window just before Daddy drove off. She heard once more her brother William, whose goodbye was advising Daddy to pay for only two weeks, because Deb would be back by then. "Never," she whispered to herself. Even so, with pounding heart, quivering hands, and tears about to spill, she followed her dad to the car. He opened the door to the blue Ford Galaxy, the first big purchase after the war. Of course, it was unlocked. Jacob Jernigan thought that the last thief had died on the cross beside Jesus. Nevertheless, through the years he had lost less than his neighbors who locked and barred. During the business of registration, he had been the old Jacob, who met a stranger with a smile and left him with a pat on the back or a handshake. Now a heavy silence hung between them. Deborah struggled to hide her tears and to find the right words—afraid to say too much—afraid to say too little. Jacob Jernigan sensed his child's dilemma. He wrapped his strong arms around her and whispered, "I leave you in God's hands." Kissing her gently on the cheek, he slid quickly behind the wheel. She watched the car round the fountain where Pallas Athena now eyed retreating cars empty of their precious cargo. The great goddess held the olive branch. "Peace be with you my father," Deborah breathed. "And peace be with me also," she finished.

Eyes on her feet, she walked slowly down the long hall and turned the corner to Room 16, home for the next nine months. Opening the door softly, she surveyed her domain. Two twin beds, two matching desks, two closets, two chests of drawers, two bare windows overlooking a tennis court. What would this anonymous roommate be like with whom she would share this cell-like space? Was this Deborah Jernigan, the persona created during countless midnight hours—the Deborah, bright, self-confident, intrepid—or was the person standing in this spartan, faceless room still Knee-deep-in-stockings listening to the titter on a Low Country bus the first day of school?

From the room next door connecting a shared bath came the sound of voices: "I think she's back."

"I bet she's a mama's girl and will cry all night."

Deborah's timid knock on the bathroom door brought a chorus of "It's open."

"Cripes! She must think we're naked."

From the doorway Deborah surveyed her suite mates. A buxom brunette with shoulder-length black curls lay on her stomach in panty and bra. In one hand she held a cigarette; in the other, an RC Cola. Her roommate, likewise clad, lay on her back fanning her toes to dry the emerald manicure just completed. Blond cropped curls and nice big blue eyes turned to the newcomer.

"Don't mind Carla. She just got out of jail and is celebrating. Grabbed a blind man's tin cup. Got only two nickels for her trouble. Not worth six months in the slammer with a year's probation, was it, Carla?"

"Liar! You are just jealous, Jackie. Anyway, I got a dollar and some change. You bet your life it was worth it. That police sergeant was one humdinger. Tucked me in every night." She dropped her burning cigarette into the empty RC from which swirled a thin line of smoke. She twirled over to view her visitor.

They were pulling her leg. Before she could respond, Carla questioned, "Hey, kid! Who made you come to a dumb school with nary a man around under fifty? Didja get a look at the faculty? The women are all great-grandmas or sex-starved old maids, and the only women the men are interested in are Helen of Troy or Cleopatra—too far away to be threatening."

"Shut up, Carla!" Jackie ordered. "We going to make our suitemate think we are a bunch of sexpots and jailbirds." Her blue eyes flashed merriment and there was gentle softness in her voice as she said, "What's your name, kiddo?"

Neither guessed that invisible hands were peeling off the knee socks with geometric patterns. What they saw was the figure of a skinny, brown-haired girl leaning carelessly on a dresser with one saddle oxford resting on an unopened locker trunk. Using an exaggerated Low Country drawl, Deborah began: "I'se Deborah Jernigan, chillen. Come frum de Big Pee Dee River where de catfish grow nine feet long and the mosquitoes big as hickory nuts. You Up Country gals ain't seen nothing in them red hills of yourn. Down home, we a right friendly folks, we is. Every Saturday night there's a dozen hoedowns at the river with free booze straight from my pappy's still to wash down the chitlings and collard greens. By nine o'clock when the wind comes from the northwest, the sheriff and his deputy won't know a handcuff

117

from a handsaw."

"God in heaven, Jackie," Carla moaned. "This ignoramus knows her Shakespeare. What was it old Miss Simpson made us learn from *Hamlet*? 'I am but mad north-northwest. When the wind is...'"

"'southerly,'" Deborah supplied, "'I know a hawk from a handsaw.'"

"Jiminy crickets, Carla, you bet me a dollar that we'd draw a dumbbell from the swamps. Looks like we got somebody who can write our themes. Pay up!" She held out her hand to Carla, who gave it a smart smack.

Suddenly the cluttered room with unmade beds and clothes thrown carelessly over furniture took on a warm glow and Mount Tabor receded into the gloom of the savannahs.

At that moment the dinner bell rang. "Deb, go grab us a table. We'll be there before the dean has a chance to bless the vittles. Jackie and I are dying to hear more about Pee Dee shenanigans. Maybe you'll take us home to one of those hoedowns."

Over supper, which would now become dinner for Deborah, she learned that her new friends were both music majors: Carla in voice; Jackie in piano. They discovered that the three were preachers' kids. Carla's and Jackie's dads were Methodists. Deborah told them her dad's favorite joke about the little boy who decided to baptize his goats; the last old billy refused to be ducked, leaving the baptizer to drop a few sprinkles on his head with a kick and an admonition: "Now go to hell with the rest of the Methodists." Following a hearty laugh, the conversation turned toward speculation of what the missing girl would be like. Deborah hoped she would be a math major. Her wish was to be granted.

Deborah cracked the window to let in an early autumn breeze. The quilt lay on the top shelf of the locker trunk. Before turning out the light, she spread it across her bed and snuggled under its warmth. With the bathroom doors open between the rooms, she listened to the conversation next door.

"You know what this room needs? A paint job."

"Really. Like what?"

"Like purple polka dots with a black swastika on the ceiling."

"Seems a bit drab to me. Suppose I sketch on the door that gal in the fountain in the front. Maybe in orange, huh?"

From next door came, "Give her a shield with snakes in one hand. That way she could keep the boogers out. Now me, I'm gonna paint my door blue. That way it will keep out the Low Country boo daddies."

"Go to sleep, Miss Smarty Pants."

Deborah smiled and felt so good. Deborah Jernigan had made a satisfactory cameo appearance on a new stage. Sleep came easily and dreamlessly. Indeed she slept so soundly that she heard nothing when during the night the missing roommate crept into the room. Only the light from the bare window facing east roused her. With her back toward the now-occupied bed, she was unaware of another presence until she saw that the window had been closed. From the corner of her eye she spied a miniature red and white jacket draped on the back of a chair.

She looked like a small animal curled beneath a plaid afghan. Only the small head crowned with silky straight black hair was visible. Her face appeared pallid as though she belonged to the ladies of another time who avoided the sun lest it mar the porcelain whiteness of their skin. She's just a big baby, Deborah thought. At any moment she will suck her thumb or reach out for someone to hold her. A strange desire to be her protector overwhelmed Deborah as she gazed at the sleeping figure that now stirred as the mouth yawned in infant innocence. It was a gentle waking. The dark eyes widened without fear.

"I'm Alexandra, the midget. But don't you dare call me Midge." There was such authority in a voice coming from one so small. "You see my dad, expecting a boy, still named me for the great conqueror. I suppose for my lack of stature." She stood on the floor and stretched to her full three feet and a half. "I don't like for people to patronize me." A laugh bubbled from her throat as she continued, "Would you like to know the prime numbers of five thousand and one?"

Deborah, who had never heard of a prime number—most of her math teachers at Union Grove had either been coaches or Home Economics teachers—answered, "Well, Alexandra, if you think my knowing prime numbers will help me pass college math, by all means enlighten me." The roommate giggled as Deborah began her formal introduction.

"My name is Deborah, the misfit. But don't you dare call me that." The two laughed together. "My father, Jacob, named me for a lady judge in the Bible because he thought my birth was a miracle. You see, I didn't cry when I was first born like other babies. My granny thought I was dead. But here I am. And here we are, Alexandra. I bet you love numbers as much as I love words. We should make a great team. You know, I hoped my roommate would be a mathematician."

"I like your name, Deborah. Let's promise each other never to shorten our names. Want to shake on it?"

A small hand clasped a brown slender one with a set of fingers coming only halfway up the brown ones. Their laugh was spontaneous. "Mutt and Jeff, huh?" Alexandra suggested.

"No way. Not even nicknames. Remember. Alexandra and Deborah."

And so it was. When the two joined Jackie and Carla at breakfast, Deborah announced, "Jackie, Carla, this is Alexandra, my roommate, who loves prime numbers like Italians like spaghetti, like Deborah likes Shakespeare, like Jackie and Carla like Chopin."

"Like Jackie and Carla like bacon," Carla added. "You see, we've already eaten it all."

"Shame on you, two," Alexandra chortled. "This way I'll never grow." General laughter followed while Alexandra dropped her cushion in her chair. Deborah looked at her three friends and around the dining room at tables filled with other green freshmen. Some were eating silently; others, chatting occasionally, but

120

none, Deborah thought, shared the camaraderie of their table. A warmth like the taste of brandy suffused her whole being. It was enough to make one believe in heaven, right here on earth. Deborah bowed her head over her plate and prayed silently, "Thank you, Jacob."

CHAPTER

Seventeen

SCHOOL DAZE

Deborah Jernigan had been a citizen of two worlds. First there were the flatlands where ancient oaks edged the Great Pee Dee and flung their mossy beards over the still water. No grass grew among their roots which spread their gnarled bones above the dark earth. On occasions children jumped miniature trestles as their fathers dangled fishing canes baited with earthworms to lure a bream as flat as the terrain it inhabited. Deborah found no play along the shore. Instead she used a fishing excursion with her father to transform the Low Country to that second world as she visited the Seven Hills of Rome or boarded the barge with Cleopatra floating down the perfumed Nile to meet her Anthony. Jacob Jernigan's gentle reprimand scarcely stirred her as her forgotten fishing pole tugged by a cruising crappie drifted downstream and snagged on a cypress knee. A book, she had learned like Emily Dickinson, was a frigate to transport her from Mount Tabor, where she could take up a new residence. And so the "compleat angler" fished not with a rod but with words. Even on a cloudy day, sunlight filtered through towering pine to highlight the page of a new world. Now with some trepidation, she sat within the ivy walls of her new home, surrounded by new faces, all appearing self-assured and completely at ease.

"God in heaven," she whispered horrified, "I am already lost," as she watched the algebra professor string an equation across a blackboard five feet wide. Of course, she had read of Archimedes and his pi and had made by Union Grove standards top grades in math. And in French class. Yet her pronunciation had sent titters around the classroom and a frown on Madame LeCerf's face. And who would believe that an earthworm pinned to a waxed tray would follow her from the peaceful Pee Dee to the biology lab. Of course, in English class, she could neither spell nor define the word *onomatopoeia*. For the first time in her life she welcomed the Holy Bible and felt quite at home as Professor Webber outlined the semester course in Old Testament. When he called her name in class and asked if she knew of the famous Deborah, her answer was worthy of a biblical scholar. "Thank you, Jacob," she murmured.

Within a few days she knew she had met her nemesis in algebra and found herself bargaining with the dean to substitute two foreign languages for one year of math. Alexandra, who had tried to drop any language for every math course the curriculum offered, yelled "Unfair!" Thus the misfit from Mount Tabor found academia not so formidable as she had imagined and took great pleasure sending home the first semester report marked *Dean's List*. Visits home were infrequent while vacations seemed interminable. Indeed, the black and white world of the past receded as she found new horizons beyond the college walls. She watched at the township auditorium Rubenstein's fingers translate Chopin poetry, Marian Anderson's open throat render German Lieder, and Toscanini's baton recreate Tchaikovsky's despair.

The world of art was no less instructive than the people around her. With new friends she burned the midnight oil and celebrated the end of exams, still wide awake with No-Doze, to play marathon bridge. They congregated to practice psychoanalysis, young Freuds interpreting dreams and asking age-old questions with no answers—only speculations that somehow drew a coterie of soul-searchers closer. Jacob Jernigan would have been horrified to hear debate on the existence of God or whether, as the philosopher had said, if he had not existed, man would have created him. Was the God of the Christian Bible the same as the one in Islam, Buddhism, and Hindu? Excluded from this so-called "intelligentsia" were the Mary Margarets, who never missed a church service and who always led the nightly vespers held on each hall. Deborah secretly envied such faith which seemed to bring peace, not turmoil to its believers. Hell's fires from Jacob's Bible had been cooled with the gentle rains of reason. They philosophically conceded that church and religion was a stabilizing force in society, establishing order through discipline, though not so stringent as the black and white world from which Deborah Jernigan had emerged.

Yet all was not order in this small girls' parochial school, though daily attendance to chapel was strictly enforced. Deborah did not mind these mild homilies but regarded them as perfunctory as grace before meals. She read of Sappho on the Isle of Lesbos and guessed that many of the famous poet's sisters lived on her hall. Real evidence, however, that "all was not right with the world" came harshly when Stella, her best friend, shook her gently on the shoulder with, "I need to talk."

"Gosh, Stella, can't it wait until morning?" she whispered, looking over at Alexander curled in the arms of Morpheus.

"I'm pregnant, Deborah."

These words were not coming from Stella Wilson, who for three years had been study companion for Dr. Browning's famous ten essay questions plus memorized English poetry. This was Stella, curly-haired Stella, whose black locks had been trained to a wavy cap that fit a sculptured head, whose large dark eyes narrowed as she unraveled abstruse meanings from Eliot's *Waste Land* or flashed with merriment as they followed the shenanigans of Fielding's *Tom Jones*—Stella, who had her life charted from a B.A. in English to a Ph.D. from the University of Chicago with perhaps a Rhodes Scholarship thrown in. How in God's name was a baby to fit into this design?

"When did you find out?"

"Tonight. Ted took me to a doctor friend. I'm two months."

"Oh, my God, Stella! You'll be dropping out of school."

"I'm not dropping out of school. I'm going to have an abortion spring break. It's all arranged."

"Abortion!" The word hissed in the darkness of the room. "You can't, Stell. That's murder. What does Ted say?"

"Murder? Who? Me? It? I can't marry until I'm twenty-one. Grandma Wilson made that condition in her will. Made a mistake herself marrying too young. Wanted to protect her favorite granddaughter. Can you see me a mother pushing a pram around an apartment complex while Ted finishes his senior year in law school? And to borrow your Low Country lingo, John and Mary Wilson would have a hissy fit. Mary might even be thrown out of the Junior League."

"I couldn't."

"Oh, yes, you could and would if you had the choice between that and going back to Mount Tabor and settling into life along the Great Pee Dee with revivals twice a year and with daily reminders that Mount Tabor's favorite daughter had dropped her sugar before the knot was tied to some reluctant mate. Yes, you would, Deborah."

"But guilt, Stella. Can you live with it? It's a life."

"Either way, there's that. Guilt for not loving a child that trapped me—guilt for not grabbing the chance to keep my life on course. Which is worse?"

The question hung in the darkness like all the others but posed heretofore by amateurs, many of whom had scarcely tasted

bitterness more than the loss of a boyfriend. This was real tragedy—as potent as Sophocles. Deborah reached for her friend, cra-
dling her head on her shoulder.

"What I want you to do, Deborah, is to invite me for spring
break. Ted's friend can arrange it in Georgetown. Then he can
drop me off at your house. Know how your mama loves to baby
you? Well, she can baby me—cook me apple pies. I might need a
little nursing, huh? Your folks will never know the difference, nor
mine neither."

Years later during their European tour, the two would remember that spring break with Anna Jernigan hovering over her
guest with a bowl of her homemade chicken soup to settle her
stomach after that food poisoning Stella had picked up in the sea-
food she had at the Waccamaw Grill. Jacob Jernigan had prayed
nightly that God would touch her body and restore her to health.
Neither would laugh as they reminisced. Neither could say that
Jacob's prayer had been answered. What Deborah knew, however, was that a kind of brooding contemplation had replaced an
infectious twinkle in her friend's eyes. Even when Stella Wilson
was named valedictorian at graduation, her smile seemed forced,
and Deborah Jernigan, an honor graduate also, clapped a little
too loudly as she watched her friend receive her diploma first.

There was a luncheon for parents, graduates, and faculty in
the college dining room. Jacob and Anna Jernigan were there
dressed in Sunday best. Anna was wearing a baby blue voile shirt-
waist with a pleated skirt. On her shoulder was a corsage of pink
carnations; Jacob sported a blossom in his buttonhole—memen-
tos from the college honoring parents. At their table sat Stella and
her parents, Greenville natives—a successful lawyer and a Junior
Leaguer. Neither seemed to notice when Jacob mixed his subject-
verb agreement. In truth they were taken with his friendly charm
and homespun wit. Anna, on the other hand, said very little, cutting her chicken clumsily as though a knife had not been a part
of a daily table setting. She eyed the green asparagus spears suspi-
ciously and pushed them delicately to the side, unwilling to sam-

ple a vegetable that was not on the menu of Low Country table d'hote. To Mary Wilson's polite inquiries and comments, Anna answered diffidently, frequently glancing at her daughter for approval. Not so with Jacob. When he was not bragging about his daughter's smarts, he was wandering among the faculty proclaiming his paternity. At one point he chatted with Dr. Morse, pastor of the nearby Methodist church, who had baptized Deborah the week before. Southern principals of schools were interested not only in academic qualifications but also in church affiliations. The prospective teacher was expected to take a role in community and church life. An unbaptized candidate, however bright, might be an atheist or even worse, a communist. Deborah had solved that problem with a visit with Dr. Morse. Now she could print on her applications *Methodist* in the blank for church preference. She had not meant for Jacob Jernigan to know.

One look at her father as he rejoined them revealed the truth. Color had left his face, and his big hand shook as he raised a water glass to his lips.

"And so you were sprinkled." His words dropped the drums of doom on Deborah's ears. Like the scene in a movie the wall of the college dining room dissolved to a front porch on a day in May when the word *blasphemy* had preceded a heart attack. Deborah reached for his hand and groped to answer the quizzical expressions on faces at the table. The Episcopal Wilsons had been baptized and christened in infancy. Sprinkle to them might connote getting one's head wet during a sudden shower. Deborah could imagine the amused laughter when they discovered the cause of Jacob's alarm. They would never know that this backwoods preacher, although ignorant of their daughter's condition, had prayed for her after she had had an abortion. The irony was laughable. A five-minute ceremony in an empty church with only a best friend looking on would be no big deal to people who went to church twice a year at Christmas and Easter. To Jacob Jernigan, it meant betrayal and repudiation of his faith. His daughter, whom he had loved with all his heart, whom he had

127

defended against a neurotic mother, for whom he had sold a tract of his beloved land to pay tuition when a drought had brought no harvest—this daughter, as he had feared, had rejected his God. In his eyes the sin she had committed would be no worse than Stella's. Each had aborted—one a child; the other, God. These were Deborah's thoughts as she met her father's eyes.

At that moment she wished that she could take a pulpit and proclaim her father's goodness to that assemblage. She wanted to defend his right to believe that the true way to salvation was a born-again experience followed by a baptism in a Low Country River Jordan administered by a John the Baptist. Jernigans for generations had followed this route, had been pillars of the community, the salt of the earth. She wanted to shout that she was proud of Jacob Jernigan, who held a Phi Beta Kappa in goodness and honesty and simplicity of spirit. At the same time she wanted to rail at a society that had not taken seriously separation of church and state. Theology had no place in a public school. This sermon she dared not deliver. She could only squeeze the hand she was holding and whisper, "I love you."

It was Stella, who came to the rescue. "Mr. Jernigan, it was just something Deborah had to have on her applications to get a teaching job. It was not like joining the church." She managed a light laugh as she continued. "One of these days old Deborah will be dipped properly in the Great Pee Dee. Reason she hasn't already is that she's afraid of water."

Jacob pushed aside his dessert. "So mote it be," he said. He took a white handkerchief from his pocket and polished his gold-rimmed glasses.

"Why, Mr. Jernigan," John Wilson questioned, "are you a Master Mason?"

"I am," came the prompt reply. He had uttered the password-identifying members of the fraternal order. "Greatest institution outside of the church," he commented.

"Well, I'll be." John Wilson stopped short of the damn in deference to the preacher. "I'm a Shriner. You know we support a wonderful children's hospital in Greenville."

"I know. I haven't gone as far as you in Masonry—."

The conversation on safe ground, Deborah whispered to herself, "Thank you, God, for Free Masonry. I shall never become a Roman Catholic. Maybe I should join the Eastern Star."

And so the four years ended. As they drove around the fountain where owl-eyed Athena gazed stonily, Deborah on the back seat of the car thought, "Not even the goddess of wisdom has answers." She was tempted to ask her father Pilate's question: What is truth? She hastily rejected the idea, fearing to stir waters temporarily placid. They moved out of the city and headed south where Mount Tabor waited to welcome its first college graduate and where no one could understand why she would turn down a teaching position at Union Grove, her alma mater.

CHAPTER

Eighteen

HUCKLEBERRY HAUNTINGS

Unlike the straight-haired Jernigans, Lenora's black hair was curly. Her skin, smooth as alabaster, needed no cosmetic to enhance her natural beauty. She had married William, the elder son, hard-working and God-fearing like his father. The Jernigans were also great talkers, some even capable of spiteful tattling. It was pious Lily who had let out of the bag the cat that deprived Deborah of the prom. Lenora, on the other hand, said little and thought much. Many of the Jernigan women distanced themselves from their sister-in-law while Anna's sharp tongue was known to bring tears to the black-haired beauty. Perhaps they were a bit in awe of *LADY*, the name her brothers had given her for she dressed modestly and walked with a certain grace. In the early years not even gregarious Deborah could penetrate Lenora's reserve, although she openly aired the opinion that Lenora was the best cook in the family. Deborah, however, adored her blond-haired niece, Vivian, Lenora's firstborn, and spent most of her time when visiting Lenora playing mama to a real doll, not like Mabelline, whom Gamin had pronounced dead. The relationship between Deborah and her sister-in-law was not strained, just undeveloped. That situation was to change the summer after Deborah's graduation from college.

As the car rolled in from Columbia and the bags were unloaded and put back in her room, Deborah had never felt so lonely in her life. She found herself hating the Low Country drawl with the unpronounced final consonants as well as the grammar that she, the prospective English teacher, had mastered. So her "coners" were now pronounced "cor-ners" with the *r* prominent in pronunciation. Mount Tabor called this talk high-fallutin', and even as the family gathered to congratulate their baby sister, they laughed at her uppity language. Furthermore, they were envious. Belle demanded that each girl be given a set of Samsonite luggage equal to the set given Deborah for graduation. Lily bragged that she could make more money preaching than teaching school. Hannah, never quite recovered from the death of Emily, bemoaned the fact that she had not been given a chance to go to college. Loyal Beryl, living in Florida, was not there to defend and bolster. As Lenora and William were leaving, Lenora drew Deborah aside and whispered, "Deborah, the huckleberries are ripe. Why don't we go tomorrow?"

"O.K." Surprised and a bit reluctant, she asked, "What time?"

"Early. Before the children get up. Besides, it gets real hot early."

Early meant a little after sunrise. When the alarm went off at six-thirty, Deborah groaned, hoping to escape a few more hours with sleep. But before she could grab her blue jeans and shirt, Lenora was tapping at her window.

"Look, I brought you a little breakfast." She handed her an apple turnover. "I have a thermos of iced tea. It's too hot to drink coffee."

131

The two took the path behind the barn and headed toward the woods bordering a field of tobacco. At the edge of the wood the sun glimmered over the Jernigan fish pond, placid except for the occasional splash of a bream breakfasting on some unfortunate cricket. They paused for a moment at the waterside. A mockingbird sat on the limb of a sweet gum imitating a brown thrasher. Only nature punctuated the silence that enclosed a small, secure world. Deborah thought of Wordsworth's lines, "The holy time is quiet as a Nun/Breathless with adoration."

"Deborah, you know the French word for sea. *La mer.* I think it is so pretty. Sounds peaceful like the waves at low tide."

"Why, Lenora, that's beautiful. What you said. I was just thinking how peaceful this all is away from the noise we humans make."

"I know what you mean. Deborah, don't pay any attention to your sisters," she laughed softly. They just making noise. They can't take away anything you have. I mean what you got at school. I'm working hard so that my children can get a college education."

"I know what you mean, Lenora." Deborah placed her arm around her lightly. "Thank you, so much."

A flock of birds in formation flew toward the woods. "Looks like the birds are going to beat us to the berries. Course I spec' there is enough for both of us."

They rounded the pond and stepped into the shadows of the woods. It was a green wood except for the bushes randomly scattered black with berries. Deborah had never been much of a berry picker, but this morning seemed special.

"You take this bush, Deborah. It's loaded. No, don't try to pick them one by one. Hold your bucket underneath and strip the stems. Only a few are still green. Yes, that's the way. If I don't stop talking, you're going to fill your bucket first."

"Don't worry. I like your kind of talk. You've always been so quiet—untalkative if that's a word."

"You have to have somebody to talk to. If you don't, it's just noise."

"How right you are."

There followed a silence broken by the gentle *plump* of berries in the lard can pails that they both carried. Deborah found herself stuffing handfuls in her mouth, the generous juices bluing her lips. The small blacker berries were the sweeter—a raw product of nature.

"Lenora, you know Mark Twain named his famous book after these berries. Huckleberry was a little boy, uncultivated like these berries. Didn't like the noise of humans either. Was happiest when he was away from people. He loved being out on the river. Made him feel free."

"Lots of times I'd like to get away, too. You know, I'd like to be a pupil in your English class."

For the second time Deborah thanked her sister-in-law. Strange, she thought, how you can live next door to a person for years and one day you are surprised to find a friend and ally. Lenora's next words echoed her thoughts.

"Deborah, William has talked with the school board about giving you a job at Union Grove. I tried to tell him that he should not meddle in your business. You can't tell some Jernigans anything."

"I can't, Lenora. I just can't. I love Daddy and Mama but..."

"You got to love yourself some, too. You didn't fight to go to college to come home to Union Grove. Ain't anything here for you."

"So you knew, Lenora. You never said."

"I don't butt in often. Last night I thought it was time to speak up. Huckleberrying was a good excuse."

"Look, Lenora, may I come over just to talk sometime? I know you're busy what with the children and everything. If you could just let me know."

The smile that touched her face reached her eyes. "We'll find time to go huckleberrying, bean picking, or even fishing down here. It's kind of nice around the pond early in the morning before the kids get up. Gives a body time to think."

"I'm not much for fishing. Daddy can tell you that."

"I ain't talking about catching. I'm talking about looking, listening, and thinking. You know what I mean? Kind of eases up on the scaredness. Sometimes a deer or two join me."

"Yes, I do know. Lenora, I'm scared to death about my future. Too bad we didn't start fishing together earlier. Seems like we've wasted a lot of time."

Deborah's basket was only half full. Somehow her hands had forgotten to pick. Lenora tipped the top of her bucket into Deborah's, equalizing their harvest. "I best be getting back. The kids will be awake."

They strolled together wordlessly, taking a new route through the woods to the road. At one point Deborah snagged her arm on a brier berry bush that drew a hint of blood.

"That's life—a prick here and there." Lenora smiled as she dabbed the wound with a clean handkerchief tucked in the pocket of her apron.

"Lenora, will you tell me sometime what makes you scared?"

"Maybe," she said as her feet turned to her little house with waking children and her husband, William, up hours before sunrise, calculating the growth of his crop and the money it would bring that would perhaps turn their simple dwelling into a comfortable home.

That long, hot summer as Deborah waited daily for answers to her applications, she spent many late afternoons shelling butter beans with Lenora, as the two became "fishing companions."

It was a relationship that would last for years until Lenora succumbed to kidney cancer. Deborah liked to think that Lenora had reached La Mer and was at peace "with the waves at low tide."

CHAPTER

Nineteen

MISS JERNIGAN, MAY I?

Pocotaligo, Yemassee, Coosawhatchie, names of former Indian villages, crisscrossed the boundary between South Carolina and Georgia. In early times indigo and rice supported the plantation and middle class communities whose rural houses nested among live oaks draped in moss. Now lumber, truck farming, canneries for surplus crops as well as oysters and shrimp provided income for black and white. A few history buffs and some curious tourists noted the former wars and massacres. Deborah had read of Gillisonville, the village where the infamous Sherman had razed every building except one residence and the Baptist Church, the headquarters of the Federals. One of the silver communion plates still bore this inscription: War of 1861 & 2 & & 4. Feb. 7, 1865. This done by a Yankee soldier. At least, Deborah thought, my first teaching assignment boasts historical importance. Not a metropolis but coastal highways lead to occa-

135

sional movies in Beaufort and shopping sprees in Savannah. She had turned to Scripture to defend her reason for turning down Union Grove's offer. "A prophet hath no honor in his own country." Jacob, who had seen the handwriting on the wall since the "sprinkling," acquiesced silently. Anna was more vocal and tearful. She couldn't understand why her daughter would turn down free board and transportation and being close to her family. Despite Anna's lamentations that Deborah's lack of driving experience would land her in some country ditch where she would be molested by an escaped convict (and Anna hadn't even read Flannery O'Connor's "A Good Man Is Hard to Find"), Jacob lent his daughter the money to buy a vintage two-door green Buick that even had an automatic shift. As soon as Deborah could hold it in the road straight and make a ninety-degree turn, she applied for a license. She scored one hundred on the written test but flunked parallel parking miserably. Archie, the patrolman, the same Archie who dubbed her Knee-deep-in-stockings, made his peace with her by giving her a license. With a twinkle in his eyes and a tip of his patrolman's cap, he bade her good-bye with "Miss Jernigan, drive careful." Only then could she laugh as she relived that bus drive to school where she had been christened and baptized with her own tears.

Two days before Labor Day weekend, with her car packed with clothes and books, Deborah Jernigan waved good-bye to her parents, standing side by side at the gate, as austere as a primitive Wood painting. Only her hands that gripped the steering wheel gave evidence of prickling fear as she launched on her first solo long drive. She did not look back but kept her eyes on the road, occasionally patting the open map at her side that would guide her to her destination.

The route took her through flat land with the road bordered with tall pine trees standing sentinel to the lone driver. September first being the opening of the deer season, she passed pickup trucks parked in clearings and occasionally sighted a hunter in camouflage garb with a rifle slung over his shoulder. Once a five-point buck leaped across the road, narrowly missing the car, escaping one calamity only to be lured perhaps into the crosshairs of a twelve-gauge shotgun.

Indian Cove High School had not been a first choice. The schools where she might have been accepted were too close to Mount Tabor and only a short ride for weekend visits. And she would know what to expect in a country school, having been a product of one. This would be a challenge. When she wrote her memoirs as an old lady, Indian Cove might add a spot of color. And who knew? There might be an eccentric young recluse living in an antebellum house who might want to share his library. It would just be her luck to be courted by a redneck looking to find a young schoolteacher whose salary would supplement his meager income. Watch out for that, she thought, and laughed aloud. It was high time for a little social life. Who would believe that a twenty-two year old had never had a boyfriend? She was ready to be swept off her feet, but she intended landing on safe ground to follow her career. Like for her friend, Stella, advanced degrees in English were somewhere up the road; unlike Stella, she did not have the means to finance them. There would be a way. And somewhere in the road ahead, there might be a home with a mate who preferred brains to beauty.

Well, she had a good figure, and the acne of adolescence had not pocked her face. Still, she was no Marilyn Monroe, but the guy she was looking for would want more than a blond bomb and buxom bosom. Such were her thoughts as she turned into the school yard marked Indian Cove Consolidated School: Home of the Tomahawks.

With that kind of introduction, she fully expected Mr. Boykin to be a red-faced Brave with feathered headgear. Instead, he wore a yellow sports shirt hanging loosely over khaki pants. *Miami Beach* in bold black letters on the front announced a recent visit. Perspiration beaded his premature bald head, and his smile revealed teeth that had been neglected. One of those vets who went to school on the GI Bill, she surmised. He probably has a

master's degree in education and was formerly a physical education teacher. Bet he's right out there with those Tomahawks every
practice. Her mental analysis of her boss was interrupted by "Is
you the new English teacher?"

She was tempted to say, "I is." She thought of answering formally with "This is she," letting him know that her English was
different from his. No use making an enemy with uppity speech,
as Mount Tabor would say. So proffering a hand with manicured
nails and bearing the gold ring of her alma mater, she responded,
"You're looking at her."

His eyes traveled down her tailored pink suit to her three-
inch white pumps. "I hope he's married," she thought silently.
His next words proved, despite his grammar, that he was a good
guy and that his lasciviousness would be confined to looking, not
exploring.

"I'm pleased to meetcha. Indian Cove's been needing a good
teacher. With your credentials you must know your stuff. Sit
down, Miss Jernigan. Can I call you Debbie?"

"Of course, Mr. Boykin." I might as well establish a formal
relationship right now, she thought, as she surveyed a cluttered
desk with papers under various weights but some still flapping
under the overhead fan.

"Well, no use fooling around on a hot day like this. Best
get down to brass tacks. You gonna be teaching six classes—seven
through twelve. I reckon I may as well warn you now. Last year's
teacher quit in the middle of the year. She couldn't handle these
younguns. You gonna have to use the paddle to make them respect you. The whip is the only thing they know." Creased anxiety
on his new teacher's face made him add hastily, "I don't mean
every day, Debbie. You just got to let them know you're boss.
One or two paddlings will spread like wildfire. These is good kids.
They just ain't had much opportunity like myself. If it hadn't
been for Uncle Sam, I'd never put foot in a college door. Forget
all that junk you learned in education. Before you can learn 'em,
you got to make 'em behave and respect you. As I said, they good

138

kids. And I'll help you." He picked up a paperweight and turned it toward her. *The buck stops here.*

It was not often that Deborah Jernigan was speechless. Six classes and the strap had unsettled her. Oh, Miss Agatha! Was I the scapegoat on that first day of school to establish order in a first grade class? "Jacob, I need your advice."

"Debbie," he said gently, "you can do it. I can see you got grit, and there's gonna be one or two who gonna test your spunk. But there's gonna be a whole bunch just waiting to love poetry and to learn how to speak correct. Don't ever let 'em know you scared. If you do, you're a goner. The old teachers will take you under their wings, just like Miss Leila where you gonna board."

Miss Leila, as the children called her, lived in a squat two-bed-room, one-bath house in a grove of pecan trees. Her stature, as compact as her dwelling, measured not over five feet and weighed in around one hundred and fifty. Patting her ample stomach, she informed her new boarder, whom she would later call Honey-bunch, that boiled peanuts and buttermilk was her favorite snack but was an enemy to her schoolgirl figure. A mass of snow-white hair framed large blue eyes that Deborah imagined twinkled even in her sleep. Her speech was intriguing. Unlike Mr. Boykin, she spoke grammatically and rapidly, but her full stops were dragged out as if she were reluctant to let that final syllable go. Leila, at sixty, and not too far from retirement from fifth grade, had the exuberance of a teenager, the humor of a comedian, and the wis-dom of a Socrates. Even before Deborah saw her tiny bedroom just large enough for a bed, dresser, and desk, she knew she had found a home as she and her housemate laughed at Mr. Boykin's grammar. They decided that he was just a good old country boy whose heart was so big that one could forgive what came out of his mouth. In fact, as Deborah was to confide later, his language smacked of Mount Tabor, though there was a slight variation in the drawl.

On that first day of school, aware of the ninety-degree weath-er, Deborah abandoned a two-piece linen suit for a black-checkered skirt and sleeveless white blouse. Leila shook her head no-no to the black patent leather heels, advising that feet at the end of a school day would be grateful for flat sandals without nylon stockings. The outfit did not conform to the new teacher's idea of professional attire; still when she saw one of her colleagues whose hair was in pink Styrofoam rollers, Deborah felt a bit over-dressed.

As the ninth grade class filed into Room 5, the new school marm stood at the door flashing a bright smile and issuing a cheery good morning. When the last scholar had scrambled to his seat, she faced her charges with "My name is Miss Jernigan." She turned her back to write her name on the now bare black-board and heard quite clearly a voice in the back of the room say, "We ain't had no English teacher last year and looks like we ain't got no better this year." An eerie silence settled over the class as they waited to hear a response.

Pretending she had heard nothing, she continued writing her full name. On the left of the classroom ran a row of six windows, each equipped with a tan sunshade with a pull. They had been carefully drawn to a uniform half-mast to break the early morning glare. As she printed the last *n* in her name, a sharp report from the back of the room announced that some hand had yanked a pull, sending the shade flying to the top. It had come sooner than she expected. Calmness masked the face that she turned toward the class. In a low, authoritative voice with each word measured and clearly enunciated, she announced, "I do not tolerate such behavior; someone has just demonstrated bad manners."

Thirty pairs of eyes scrutinized her. For at least thirty seconds, no one stirred. Then a freckle-faced girl in blue overalls and red shirt sitting in the front desk nearest to the window leaned over and hooked the rounded end of the pull with her index finger sending the shade skyrocketing to join its twin on the back window.

Deborah heard two voices: First, Mr. Boykin. "The only thing they know how to respect is the whip. Don't let them see you're scared. If you do, you're a goner." The second one was Saint Paul in the mouth of her father, Jacob Jernigan. "Spare the rod and spoil the child." Every fiber of her being rebelled at such admonition. Methods classes in discipline had not recommended such measures, and certainly the students in advanced classes whom she had in practice teaching had never challenged her authority. "To survive or not to survive is the question," she muttered silently.

Opening the top drawer on the left side of the desk, she drew out a paddle. In an ironic twist of fate, someone had scratched Board of Education in red letters. She walked slowly to the offender's desk. "Stand please and bend over or face double punishment with Mr. Boykin with me looking on." To her surprise and relief, the miscreant stood, turned her posterior to the paddle and braced herself with her hands on the desk. Both hands delivered three sharp whacks. "You may now sit, young lady." Moving back to her desk, Deborah picked up the text *Literature and Life* and turned to O'Henry's "The Ransom of Red Chief."

"Class, I love to read and I especially love to read to others. Here is one of my favorite stories about a very lovable but mischievous young scamp who outwitted his kidnappers. I hope that this year I can share many of my favorite stories with you." Pulling an empty front desk forward and turning it to face the class, she sat down and began. The performance was worthy of an Oscar. Her voice played each of the characters as her eyes made intermittent contact with her audience. Within a few minutes she knew she had them. She had won. The bell rang thirty minutes later. No one moved. Somebody said, "Darn it all. We ain't gonna know what happened."

"Oh, yes, you will. That's your assignment for tonight. It's on page 201 in your literature book." She rose to open the door and watch ninth grade English file past. A boy as redheaded as the character about whom she had been reading grinned at his new teacher and whispered, "You sho read good."

"Thank you," she whispered back. "Thank you, Jacob, thank

141

you, God, thank you everybody," she said aloud as she turned to the empty classroom, adjusted the two shades, and took a breather until her next class forty-five minutes away.

Driving home with her housemate in late afternoon, Leila was bubbling with laughter. "Well, Miss Jernigan, the news spread all the way to grammar school by ten o'clock. We just tickled to death. I would give a plugged penny to have been a fly on the wall. And that brat of Joe Driscoll's got the licking. You know what I think? This calls for a cel-e-bra-tion." She drew out each syllable in exaggerated drawl. "It's time for me to get out my bottle of Jack Daniels I've been saving for a special occasion and mix us an Old Fashion."

And so they did. They had not one but two before they sat down to leftover roast and vegetables. Without a care in the world the new teacher slipped in between crisp starched sheets. As a cool night wind drifted through the open window, she dreamed she was floating around her classroom riding a paddle instead of a broomstick while quoting Shakespeare: "All the world's a stage,/And all the men and women merely players."

"Necessity is the mother of invention" was the adage that guided her through the first year of teaching. She found methods that never made it into a teacher's manual. She taught them to find verbs in a sentence by prefacing *I, you, we, they*. One day a seventh grader called *we* a verb. As she chanted the conjugation, the class burst into peals of laughter with *we we*. Suddenly realizing that she was announcing a communal trip to the bathroom, she, too, joined in their mirth. She would never forget the day when she saw tears in eyes as she recreated the midnight parting of *Romeo and Juliet*. All her life she treasured a copy of an essay written by one of her pupils on "The Teacher Who Made the English Language Beautiful."

Outside the classroom she enjoyed the companionship of her neighbors—some farmers, some sawmill workers, some teachers—none with whom she shared Dostoevsky or Keats, but all exhibiting dignity and goodness, heroes and heroines worthy of the great literary prototypes. She dated Lanier, who hauled lumber for International Paper, who had never heard of the poet by the same name who had made the marshes and rivers of the South into medleys as smooth as the music of the flute that he played. Toward the end of the year, it was Lanier who escorted her to call upon a student whose mother had died of cancer, and for the first time in her life, Deborah Jernigan fainted.

Olivia Gardner was the brightest pupil in eleventh grade English. A voracious reader who had exhausted Indian Cove's meager library, she had a facility with words that sprang from a keen ear for refined language, an innate talent reincarnated, no doubt, from some unknown ancestor. She was just a wisp of a girl who wore homemade cotton dresses faded from frequent washings but always looking freshly laundered. Deborah scarcely noticed her scant wardrobe. Her big brown eyes made one forget her other facial features. She saw those eyes register pleasure at a well-turned phrase or sadness as she relived a *Hamlet* or an *Antigone*. Deborah could not guess until the night after Olivia's mother died, that this sensitive child, who had sat in her class almost nine months, had not been experiencing great drama vicariously, but was living it daily as tragic as any written by Sophocles.

Everyone tried to dissuade her from paying a visit to Olivia's home. Wise Leila foretold Olivia's embarrassment to have her teacher see the Gardner poverty. "I'm not going to judge their housing conditions. I'm going to see one of my favorite and brightest students whose mother has died. Olivia would understand that. She knows I am not judgmental. Anyway, I have seen people living in shacks. Remember, I am a Southerner."

Lanier picked her up. First they would make a brief call at the Gardeners. Then they would go to Beaufort for a movie. Just before they turned down a dirt lane, Lanier stopped the car. "Deborah," he questioned for the third time, "are you sure you want to do this? The body is at home, not in a funeral home."

"Of course! People in Mount Tabor bring the coffin home for the wake."

It was a very warm night. Dusk had fallen, and without electric lights the Gardener home hulked above a junkyard of cars. Lanier's supporting arm helped her up the step—one concrete block to a sagging plank porch with wooden shutters gaping at the darkness. The open door led into what might have been any room but was now devoid of furniture except for a table along with benches and a few wooden chairs lining the walls. A single kerosene lamp on the square table in the center of the room cast faint shadows upon the occupants. On one bench lay Olivia's mother awaiting a coffin to be provided by the county welfare for the indigent. A single sheet covered the body except for the head. Straight black bangs fringed the closed eyes and fell into twin lifeless locks framing the pallid face, an incongruous youthful pageboy arranged in grotesque defiance of death. Deborah wondered if the marble lids encased large brown eyes like her daughter's and if in better days they had flashed in merriment. A man, presumably the husband, sat next to his wife. He was lifting a halfpint of Old Crow to his whiskered lips and taking no notice of the callers. On the opposite side of the room sat two men, one a guard, puffing on a cigar and handcuffed to a young man wearing horizontal black and white stripes, the uniform of the chain gang. A black stubble covered his shaved head bowed to the bare pine floor. No one rose; no one spoke. Olivia was nowhere in sight. The stench of smoke, corn liquor, and an unembalmed body, dead for twenty-four hours, pervaded the airless room. Deborah clamped her eyes to shut out the wasteland before her. The next thing she remembered, she was back in the car. Lanier was slapping her cheek and calling her name.

"What happened, Lanier?"

"You fainted, Miss Jernigan. Good thing I was there to catch you. You might have fallen on Mrs. Gardener. That would make a story for the Beaufort paper. Maybe even the *Charleston News and Courier*."

"Don't joke, Lanier. It's too awful for words. Take me home. What I need is one of Leila's drinks."

"What you need is a paddling for going in the first place. That might make the papers, too. *Local Boy Paddles Teacher.*" Drawing her close, he kissed her gently.

Neither his humor nor affection could dim the horror she had witnessed. How awful to face Olivia Monday, she thought.

But Olivia did not return to school. It was the end of the term and Deborah's last week at Indian Cove. "Has my work been finished?" she pondered. "I sound like my father with the zeal of a Baptist preacher called to save souls," she mused, smiling to herself. "Jacob's blood is in my veins. But lately, Daddy, I have had a transfusion. Must I always be an apostle to the deprived and hopeless Olivias?" With a work fellowship and scholarship she would head to the University to start on a master's degree in English. On Olivia's report card that she left at the school, she wrote: *Olivia, you were my shining light this year. You have a future in languages. Miss Leila will give you my address if you want me to write recommendations.* She added mentally, "Forgive me, Olivia." She never saw or heard from her again.

CHAPTER

Twenty

A LIBERAL EDUCATION

T here is no doubt that the Deep South offers refuge to those fleeing inclement winters in the North. No so with summer. Before the advent of air-conditioning, those below the Mason-Dixon Line sweltered as the thermometer frequently tipped one hundred with humidity just short of that mark. Eggs could fry on asphalt streets; bathers without sunscreen blistered even under cloudy skies; electric fans simply stirred hot air. It is no wonder that Southerners move slowly and lethargically. Not even winter stirs them out of their torpor. The summer when Deborah matriculated in the graduate school at the University, the mercury set records. Each morning she left a sodden outline of her body on her bed in the women's dormitory. The carrel assigned to her in the basement of the library became a cubicle in Dante's *Inferno*. It was no wonder that she rapidly developed aversion to Seventeenth Century Prose and Poetry and to Dr.

Tim Littlejohn, who taught the course.

He could not have been named more appropriately, for he was a runt of a man in double-breasted suits, bow ties, and baggy pants, his daily apparel regardless of the temperature. His voice just escaped a squeak, and if he could sing, Deborah imagined his range would be somewhere between a lyric soprano and a coloratura. Certainly his rendering of poetry would have made Donne and Marvel plug their ears. Even so, such pieces as "To His Coy Mistress" animated his voice to an even higher treble. His eyes were his most prominent feature—two big brown orbs bulging behind gold-rimmed spectacles that scrutinized his charges as well as their papers, checking every footnote right down to the accuracy of the page in the citation. Rumor had it that he had been happiest as a lowly private in the army, an MP who directed traffic from the posts where he was stationed and where he was quite content that his tenure in service was confined to the home front. His Mama with higher aspirations for her son who had scored phenomenally high on the Graduate Record Exam steered him into academia. Now he directed students through the prolixity of Burton's *Anatomy of Melancholy* and Donne's erudite sermons.

And so it was that Deborah with wet brow and eyes blinded with sweat, not tears, sat on a hot July night in her carrel, checking the last reference on a paper she had written on conceits in Donne's poetry, when a warm hand lightly touched her shoulder. Hot as it was, a cold chill like the charge of an electric current, spun her around to face Dr. Littlejohn.

"You scared me to death, Dr. Littlejohn.'

"I see you are working hard, Deborah." It was the first time he had called her by her given name. He maintained the strictest formality in his classes. Why the sudden familiarity? What could she possibly say to this man who bored her to death in class, tortured her with weekly papers, and assigned tomes of nightly readings of the driest prose in the English language?

"Yes, I am," she managed weakly. "What are you doing out

on such a hot night, Dr. Littlejohn? Surely you are not doing research for a paper? Maybe you're just checking up on students to see if they are keeping their noses to the grindstone," she quipped.

"No. Neither. Why don't you call me Tim, Deborah? It's all right out of class to drop formalities. Besides I've been wanting to talk to you for some time."

"My work? It's not satisfactory? I know I haven't shown much enthusiasm for the course, but I've tried to do the assignments."

"Your work is fine—analytically exemplary." To her surprise he laughed as he said, "Who could be enthusiastic about the *Areopagitica*? I bet Milton was bored himself."

"You mean...?"

"Of course, I would prefer teaching Shakespeare or Keats. It would be quite an incongruity—my teaching Romantics. Don't you agree? Seventeenth century goes with the personality."

Why was he telling her this? A professor doesn't get personal so suddenly without reason. Not even Dr. Browning, whom she had adored, with whom she had had warm chats—but never had he talked in such a revealing way. The desk light glimmered on the glasses of the little man beside her. Was there softness in those otherwise penetrating eyes? His next words threw new light on this sudden intimacy.

"Bob, your creative writing teacher, shared your sketch on Knee-deep-in-stockings. I thought I would like to get to know the writer better. You don't have to answer this, but was it autobiographical?"

"Yes, Tim, it was. Of course, I embellished the details a bit."

"Know what I was called? *Four eyes*. And after Miss Clark read us *The Christmas Carol*, I was rechristened *Tiny Tim*. Even the high school principal, who handed me my diploma, congratulated *Tiny Tim*."

Their laughter mingled. Three carrels away somebody issued a "Shush."

In a whisper Deborah said, "Tiny Tim, meet Knee-deep-in-stockings," as she proffered her hand.

"Want to walk down to the Wade Hampton Hotel and have a Coke? It's air-conditioned. I sometimes grade papers in a corner of the lobby."

As they ambled down the street, Deborah found herself telling him about Alexandra, her college roommate, the midget with a genius IQ who loved prime numbers the way Deborah loved words. "We were Mutt and Jeff," she said, "but neither of us used that term."

Over a Coke, Tim's brown eyes met hers. There was actually a twinkle in them. "Guess what. I don't mind being Mutt so long as you will be Jeff." His words were soft absent the squeak. "Deborah, I don't mean anything out of the way." The professor was groping for his words. "There are so few one can talk to. Friends are important. Even before I read your paper, I thought I had met a kindred spirit. Tonight I followed you to the library. It took me two hours to get up the nerve." He shook the ice cubes gently in his empty glass. "I'm glad I did."

"I'm glad you did, too, Tim."

It was the beginning of a friendship that would last for years. She did not mind being teased about her professor boyfriend, who coached her for orals, and who understood the ambivalence of daughter to father. She toyed with the idea of introducing him to Mount Tabor, and though she knew he would never reveal his unorthodox views on religion to Jacob, she did not want that black-and-white world of the Bible Belt to judge him.

After that first summer at the university, she moved into a two-story Victorian house just off-campus, the residence of graduate and foreign exchange students. It was not only a place to live but also a graduate school in the study of human behavior. Deborah laughingly said that each of the residents was having an affair except her and Francine, her French roommate, a buxom blue-eyed blond mademoiselle. She was sure that many of her housemates thought she was sharing Tim's apartment in the Towers. Her chance of a liaison was not limited to Tim, for Wes, her fellow worker at the history library had propositioned her the first week.

"You lack experience, Deborah. I'm a damn good teacher. I could prepare you for the right guy when he comes along. It won't cost you a penny except your cherry," he laughed.

"I don't love you, Wes. Besides, you always smell like garlic. Sorry."

"Who said anything about love? But I'll swear off garlic so as not to offend your tender sensibilities. Bet I could turn you into one of my swamp gals in a week."

Wes had explained that his summer work took him and his tent to the backlands where he preached rousing sermons of hell fire and damnation to repentant sinners who filled his hat that was passed around with crisp bills from local tobacco markets. Some more attractive members of the opposite sex had thanked him further by bestowing more personal favors in the name of the Holy Ghost. Deborah, who prided herself on concealing her naïveté, could not pretend that she was not only shocked but also horrified.

"Wes, that's downright blasphemy. You're going straight to hell." She couldn't help smiling as she realized that this was Jacob's daughter with his words in her mouth.

"Hell? You're even dumber than I thought. You don't think I believe in all that God talk I spew out. It's the easiest way I know to put myself through graduate school. Besides, it's downright fun. That tent was the best investment I ever made."

The proposition turned down, the two worked amicably together on research and transcriptions of letters of Confederate soldiers. Deborah chalked him up as one of her learning experiences in the real world. During the year the house off-campus was to provide further enlightenment unrelated to academics.

Francine, her French roommate, shared a tiny upstairs room with a radiator that squawked all night and kept the room so hot that it would cure a barn of tobacco. In the middle of the night they would thrust open the window to let in a breath of winter air.

It reminded Deborah of home—heated by chimneys where one was likely to be burning up or freezing depending upon the proximity of the fire. The window often offered diversion from study, for it provided an unobstructed view of the football practice field. The two sometimes identified one of their housemates keeping a late night assignation. Downstairs, the widow Eunice, a major in social work, who acted as housemother to the younger residents, would rendezvous elsewhere. She would slip out the back door of her room at night and return at daybreak. One night Deborah and Francine, having heard her nocturnal departure, moved the bedside table in front of her door. On the table sat an upturned trash can topped with the vase of red roses, the love token from her secret admirer—secret to no one in the house since Maureen, a fellow graduate in social work, reported walking into Professor Womack's office and catching Eunice and the good prof in flagrante delicto. The shattering of glass and the clang of a rolling trash can accompanied Eunice's return from her love fest as she pushed opened the door ever so softly at five A.M.

"Do you suppose the roses are ruined, Francine?"

"C'est terrible,"" she returned, convulsed in laughter.

If one judged by appearances, Francine, a blowsy blond, would be the likely suspect for amours. Her healthy bust, uninhibited by a brassiere, bounced as she walked, bringing whistles and catcalls as she sashayed along, especially when she was downtown on Saturday night when soldiers were on leave from the nearby fort. Francine, turning upon a cadre of khaki, would curse them out in French and then flounce onward, leaving her startled admirers disarmed. Deborah knew exactly how Mount Tabor would size up Francine and decided that her roommate would fare no better under scrutiny than her friend, Tim. Therefore, her home was deprived of her two closest and most interesting friends. *An outward appearance doth not proclaim the man* became her new maxim.

At Christmastime when the house gathered around the chimney glowing cheerfully with oak logs contributed by Tim, the

German girl, Traudl, interrupted Yuletide carols when she burst into a Hitler youth song. Deborah and Eunice dragged away Francine whose fists reactivated French Resistance in World War II on Traudl's corpus. Maureen calmly steered her roommate into the safety of their abode across the hall.

Maureen was the epitome of the well-dressed, cultured, and conventional Southern woman. A tall, slender brunette, who wore her well-groomed hair shoulder-length, had the patronizing smile of the Old South matron and the poise of a seasoned debutante. *Class* was the word for Maureen. She walked with the assurance of a woman secure in her world. Her pleasingly pitched voice never offended. Deborah imagined that catastrophe could not alter her bearing nor shake her demeanor. There was an air of mystery, however, surrounding Maureen. Every Saturday afternoon she would pack an overnight bag, her camera, and her tripod and disappear in her blue convertible until late Sunday afternoon. Traudl reported that Maureen was visiting an ailing Aunt Martha, who had a chateau overlooking Lake Murray. In such riparian surroundings, Deborah surmised she captured beautiful sunsets or a rare bald eagle in her camera lens.

One afternoon Maureen way-laid Deborah who was heading upstairs. She asked her to come in for a cup of tea. Maureen heated the water on a hot plate but served the tea grandly from a miniature Sheffield silver service. Deborah had never tasted hot tea without lemon, and that afternoon Maureen introduced her to the English way with cream and two lumps of sugar. With a hand holding the bone china cup with two fingers and the others poised outward at just the right angle, Maureen asked, "Deborah, would you like to see my photograph album?"

"Why, I'd love to. I bet you have some beautiful shots of that lake."

Maureen smiled and, placing her cup on the silver tray, she rose. "My pictures do capture nature. A special kind."

She removed a heavy album from a nearby bookcase and, settling herself on the bed, she motioned Deborah to join her.

Scrolled in white letters on the blank black page was the caption: *The Feet of the Undefeated.* Just as Deborah was about to tell her that she had misspelled a word, Maureen turned the page. There were two pairs of feet positioned side by side with only a portion of legs below the knees exposed. Under the feet on the right, the name *Ted* was inscribed in white ink. Beneath the name in smaller print was a date.

Maureen turned the page. Another set of feet. This time the name under the right set was *John* with a date. There followed page after page and name after name and date after date with no name ever repeated. Not even Wes's tent meetings had been so shocking.

"Do you want to see more?" The voice, poised, modulated as always, continued. "Aunt Martha is presently residing at Fort Jackson. We dine at the Officers' Club on Saturday night. You can see, Deborah, that the caption is not misspelled," she finished matter-of-factly.

At that moment Traudl bustled in the room with an armful of books that she dropped on her empty twin bed. "What have you two been up to?" she questioned.

"Looking at pictures," Maureen returned.

Still not speaking, Deborah found her way to the door. She managed to say, "Thank you for the tea." As she opened the door, Maureen laid a hand on her shoulder and said softly, quoting *Hamlet*: "'There are more things in heaven and earth, Horatio, than are dreamt of in your philosophy.'"

Back in her room Deborah pondered why Maureen had chosen her. Why had she singled her out like the ancient mariner who had detained the wedding guest? Was it just amusement in shocking the unworldly? She wondered what Jacob would say. Some day she might share her experience with him. No, she decided. Such did not fit in Jacob's philosophy. Nor hers neither. As the first reaction subsided, her thoughts turned back to Maureen. Who was she? What drove her to these strange episodes, carefully planned with tripod and remote control camera in place? The questions remained unanswered, and neither she nor Maureen ever alluded to the afternoon tea.

One rainy, foggy Sunday night, a policeman sighted an overturned blue convertible aflame off Highway 1. Weeks later, Aunt Martha, wearing serviceable tweeds, her gray hair a perfect coiffure, appeared at the house to claim Maureen's belongings. The album would have been among them except its ashes lay curled under a half-burned log in the chimney of the downstairs general room. Deborah wondered how many had shared Maureen's album. Now it would be safe from prying eyes.

At night when Deborah was too exhausted either to sleep or to study, she lay in the darkness of the house under whose roof such divergent souls slept, and thought. *Love*. She could hear the words of broken Othello as he wept over his guiltless wife whom he had strangled: *It is the cause, my soul; it is the cause*. Its absence or presence so often ended in tragedy. There was Maureen, who died seeking it; and Tim, afraid to search for it; Cousin Hester, who rode away in a red pickup truck to find it; and even Anna, her mother, unaware that she had it. Last Christmas Anna had given each of her children, except Deborah, a baby doll wearing identical dresses painstakingly tucked and tatted into replicas of her wedding gown. There were others like little Ling from Formosa, desperately in love with an American doctoral candidate, deprived of it because of family opposition. Even Wes, brilliant and arrogant, denied the need of it. And Deborah? Cupid's arrow had not wounded her. Yet she dreamed of it, but even in her midnight reveries, there was a sense of something not quite right, a kind of foreboding that could break profound slumber with fear. Once she talked to Tim about it.

"Tim, have you ever been in love?" They were sitting on a bench on the campus feeding birds. It was the mating season. Once, cardinals had built a nest in the thicket of a Carolina Cherry under her window. The protection of the mate as he flew guardian around the nest charmed her, and she wondered if they mated for life.

"Many times, Deborah. Once in particular. You know, I'm another Somerset Maugham. My loves have all been unrequited."

"I'm sorry."

"Don't be." He tossed a handful of seed to waiting feather friends. "Love is more dangerous than alcohol. And you?"

'No, not really. I'm a bit afraid. You know my father says he loves God with all his heart, mind, and soul. It's hard to love the invisible, don't you think?"

"I don't know, Deborah. Your father's love for the Almighty is different from the kind we want. His kind is safer and reassuring. We humans are prone to indulge in fantasy. I sometimes think the dream is better than the reality. It's safer anyway."

Stooping, she picked up a gray feather some migrant had dropped in flight. She held it up to the light as though it were a crystal ball to reveal the future. "But Tim, I want to live. I want to find out what love is like. Even if it doesn't last." She blew on the feather. A convenient wind swirled it earthward.

"Might be a lesson in that feather," Tim quipped in exaggerated drawl and dialect.

"Might be," she repeated as she tossed the last of the sunflower seed to two mourning doves.

And so the year ended and another hot summer lay ahead to complete a thesis that, according to the advisor, was inundated with baseless conclusions. Deborah moved back into the dormitory. Middle-aged teachers endeavoring to renew their certificates by passing music appreciation surrounded her. The final test was recognition of composer and work. Deborah had thought she would never tire of classical music, but after having heard the same recordings from the portable phonograph next door continuously, she was ready to turn to jazz or even country. It was a lonely time. Tim had taken a sabbatical and was off to Europe for a year. The house where she had lived for nine months looked as forlorn as she felt but guarded the secrets of its former occupants well.

Unlike the previous summer, it rained every day. There were few hours when the sun lifted his feeble face. Turbulent clouds obscured the stars. Omens? Only when the last page of her thesis met the approval of her advisor, who now had an unoriginal treatise copious with quotes and citations, did the weather lift. The mercury soared as the Deep South once again wilted under the bright rays of Indian summer. Deborah was broke. She needed a job. Tim had offered to finance a year in Europe where she could have time to start that novel she had always wanted to write—where in Paris she might meet a budding Hemingway or a Virginia Woolf. It would be a loan and an investment, he had said. Deborah was tempted but knew Jacob would believe that she was a kept woman and a disgrace to the Jernigans, who had led upright lives without even a divorce. Besides, Anna was ill. Jacob needed her, and so Deborah found herself teaching junior and senior English in a town only fifty miles from Mount Tabor.

CHAPTER

Twenty-One

ANNA

"Deborah, your mother's sick. I've asked the Lord for his will to be done, but this is something I don't know how to deal with. The Lord must be punishing me—something I done, something I didn't do. I've tried to live close to the Lord. I've made mistakes, I know. If this is how I have to pay, I need help to stand it." Tears trickled down his unshaven cheeks. He took off his glasses and drew a handkerchief from his sweater pocket. Wiping his tears, he continued. "The Bible says 'And God shall wipe away all tears.' I reckon that means when we leave this world. But I can't leave her. There's nobody to take care of her. You children got your own lives. I just try to live one day at a time."

He reached over and drew a Kleenex from a box and began slowly polishing his glasses. They were in the little store across the road from the house. It was here that Deborah had learned arithmetic firsthand as she learned to make change from quarters and even dimes. A can of Tube Rose snuff was only a nickel. Mount Tabor had passed through its doors carting away flour, rice, coffee, tea—those items their farms didn't produce that were essential for living—along with a few treats, RC Colas and Dr. Peppers, dopes they called them, bars of Butterfingers and Snickers and perhaps a slab of hoop cheese weighed on the scales suspended from the ceiling. Here Jacob joked with his neighbors, charged their groceries without interest until they sold cotton and tobacco, and counseled them in their troubles. Now as he sat in his rocker immured in his own woes, he questioned that sufficiency promised by his God. Deborah pulled up an empty nail keg and sat down in front of her father. She clasped both of his stubby, squat hands in hers, and looking up in his watery blue eyes she began.

"Daddy, you remember once I told you that if Baptists have saints, you would be Saint Jacob. Even Saints suffer, Daddy. Right along with the sinners. Suffering doesn't come from the God you love. If he loved enough to die for you, why would he hurt you? Oh, Daddy, suffering is the part we pay for being mortal. Remember David? In that beautiful twenty-third psalm, there is no promise of a life of green pastures beside still waters."

"What about Job? He was a good man. God let him suffer."

"To prove to the devil that Job's faith was strong. There is no question about your faith, Daddy." She would have liked to share with him the fact that Job almost didn't get into the canon of the Bible. But to question Holy Writ would be a mistake even in his time of despair. Reassurance was the better strategy.

Jacob leaned over and kissed his daughter on the cheek. It was a special moment. His grief, his doubt, his questions had brought them closer. Deborah wished that she could express her gratitude, but even though words were her forte, she knew how dangerous they could be. Love without voice and communion in silence were safer. Still it was a kind of Eucharist without the bread and wine. The clock on the counter ticked away time and returned them to the immediate.

"Your Mama's mental. I had to sell all the chickens. She can't stand to hear a rooster crow. I even have to unplug the refrigerator at night. Some nights she walks the floor wringing her hands. She don't want me to touch her. And, Deborah, she don't even want to see you, her baby."

"What do the psychiatrists say?"

"She's had shock treatment. I hated to do it. It helps for a few days. Calms her. She kind of walks around in a dream. Then it all comes back."

They needed a Jung or Freud. Deborah had always wondered what had happened in her mother's past that had turned her in to a termagant, one riddled with fear, one unnaturally possessive of her children. Now memories flooded her. Not one of her sisters had had a proper wedding. She remembered Beryl's wedding day and her mother's wails and dire pronouncements before she took to the woods. She thought of the wedding dress that she had copied for the doll, the one that she had heartlessly thrown into the fire, wreaking vengeance over the loss of a bicycle. Then there was the quilt. Her mother had painstakingly fashioned it with arthritic hands for her daughter's graduation gift. What was responsible for her secret visits to the wine bottle? How much had her baby daughter contributed to her insecurity? Bitter though it was to accept, Deborah knew that through the years, hostility had clouded her vision and cruelty had often been a substitute for understanding. A wave of guilt washed over her. There had been little doubt among the Jernigan clan that Jacob was the favored parent. How lonely must the years have been for Anna! "How could I have been so blind?" she thought.

Jacob's words brought her back to the present. "If she don't get better, there is the asylum. You know—the one on Bull Street in Columbia where they send crazy people. But your Mama's not crazy—not like Tom Warner who shot into a yard full of children at the schoolhouse. And then there was his son who stuck a stick of dynamite under his uncle's barn blowing up his mules and cows. Kind of runs in the Warner family—craziness. Been nothing like that in her family, as I know of. Anyway, she means no harm. Her mind just hurts. Asylum! I can't bear the thought of it."

"Daddy, there have to be alternatives. There are drugs for depression. Surely the doctors have suggested another course."

"They want to operate on her brain. I can't think of the big word they use. They want to cut some nerves in the front of her head. It's something new. The operation has not been performed at the Medical College of Charleston yet. And they don't guarantee anything. I'd have to sign for it. I know God can heal a diseased mind as well as a body. How long do I have to wait on him? What should I tell the doctors?"

Deborah stood and walked slowly to the door and eyed her mother's flower garden, untended now. The unstaked dahlias, heavy with blossom, sprawled on the ground. Weeds thrust themselves through chrysanthemums just beginning to bloom. Brown leaves from the oak tree splattered the upswept concrete walk. In her mind's eye, Deborah could see Lady Macbeth wringing her hands in despair and her husband questioning the doctor, "Canst thou not minister to a mind diseased?" Now sat her father, his face furrowed with pain, seeking advice from a daughter who had no answer either. At that moment she yearned for some sage who could fill her mouth with wisdom—a Mr. Fix-it, who could restore relative peace to the Jernigan household. In the absence of a miracle worker, she would have to rely on science. "Daddy, I don't think we have a choice. Lobotomy is what the doctors are suggesting. I've read about it. They will cut the nerve fibers in the frontal lobes of the brain. It is supposed to relieve tension and anxiety. Medicine has come a long way. Just think nobody has to have small pox or typhoid fever," she added reassuringly.

He braced his hands on the chair arms and rose. Deborah detected a slight hesitation as though he were afraid of falling. She reached out to steady him. His hand explored his bearded cheek. "Reckon I forgot to shave. I didn't know my college daughter was coming this early." He bestowed an artificial smile upon her as he wrapped one arm around her waist. "Let's go to the house and see your Mama. She's quieter today. She had one of them treatments recently. The doctor says she can't have any more for a while."

Although it was a pleasant autumn day, Anna lay on the bed in a summer gown with a fan on the bedside table oscillating. It blew wisps of gray hair over her closed eyes. "She's always hot," Jacob whispered.

"I ain't asleep. I told you, Jacob, I don't feel like company."

"It's Deborah, Anna. Our girl's come to spend the weekend with us. That ought to make you feel better. I'm gonna go in the kitchen to scrap up a little supper—some ham and eggs. I might make a little grits. I'll fix 'em thick the way you like 'em."

"I told you, Jacob, I ain't hungry. Ain't nothing gonna make me feel better." She opened her eyes and turned them on her daughter.

Deborah sat down on the edge of the bed. She leaned over to kiss her on the cheek. Anna turned her head abruptly away. Deborah took her mother's hand in both of hers and squeezed it. "Mama, I have been worried about you. It doesn't seem quite right not smelling your chicken frying or getting a whiff of collards in the iron pot simmering in backbone. Remember how I love those corn dodgers soaked in pot liquor?"

Anna pulled her hand away. "My collard cooking days are over. You worried about me? Your *Daddy* was always it." She emphasized the word. "Reckon you know I tried to get rid of you before you was born. It wouldn't work. Here you come, weak and puny. I lost my health trying to raise you. And I ain't never had thank you for it. Don't tell me you worried about me. And you come between me and Jacob, too. He's always taking your part against me. I'd been better off if you'd never been born."

Her words were lumps of lead, crushing her, stifling her breath. She felt no anger toward the wraith-like person beside her. She wanted to touch her—to gather up those straggling hairs blowing intermittently as the fan turned, to make order out of disorder. Neither touch nor speech was sufficient. Her next words

161

were even more searing.

"You know what I'd like to do? I'd like to take them fancy diplomas of yours and throw them in the chimney and see them burn up the way you burned my doll. I never had a real doll when I was little. Only one Ma made out of corn shucks."

Restraining herself no longer, Deborah rushed from the room. "That's right. Go to your Daddy. Just like always." Her mother's words followed her to her room where she threw herself on her bed and stuffed a pillow in her mouth to stifle the sobs that wrenched her. Never had there been such tears, acid raining on her soul. Twin monsters, rage and pity, fought for dominance—pity for the mother whom she had not loved and rage at herself who had been so blind. And now that she could offer her love, it was unwanted. Tim's words came back to her. "Love is more dangerous than alcohol." Its absence equally dangerous, she thought. Now was not time to philosophize. Jacob must not know. Jacob needed her.

They said little over supper. Deborah kept her eyes lowered in order to conceal her swollen lids. As Jacob emptied Anna's untouched plate in the garbage, he said, "Deborah, it's time to call the family together and let them know my decision. Beryl is the only one far away. You call her."

"Daddy, did the doctors say what would be the immediate effect?"

"They said it would blot out the recent past. She won't remember what she said to you today," he finished as he picked up the unwashed skillet, avoiding her gaze.

Too bad I can't have a lobotomy, too, she thought. Too bad there is no eraser to wipe the slate clean and start with a clean board.

On a gray morning in a gray waiting room, a family of gray Jernigans waited. They were all there: Lily constantly on the phone apprising her prayer group of the latest news; Hannah, lost in thought, perhaps remembering little Emily and her premature demise; Gamin and William, their childhood squabbles momentarily forgotten, passing the time by discussing the deer season; Belle, still beautiful in middle age, recounting details of a recent wedding of one of her daughters, describing to Deborah and Beryl in minute details the wedding dress she had fashioned herself: "I tried to copy Mama's. She would be so thrilled. Too bad she and Daddy couldn't come to the wedding." Deborah smiled wryly and focused her attention on Jacob, who at the moment was at the door, peering down the hall in hopes of spying a doctor. He had been making these trips to the door every five minutes or so all morning. Belle, in her saccharine concern, said, "Daddy, sit down. You know you've had a heart attack. We don't want to lose you, too." Like her mother, she always looked on the dark side.

This, too, enraged Deborah. "Belle, mind your own business. If Daddy wants to walk, let him walk. It's his heart, not yours." She was still rankling over the fuss Belle had made over the Samsonite luggage.

"Well, Miss Priss, just because you've been to college doesn't make you an authority on everything. You keep your bossing in the classroom."

"Tut, tut." Here was Jacob's gentle "Shut up."

At that moment the door opened and a doctor still in scrubs entered. Jacob jumped to his feet and met him before he could clear the door.

"It's over, Mr. Jernigan," he said, shaking Jacob's hand. "She stood the operation quite well and should be awake within an hour. I can't tell you at this point what the outcome will be except that there should be no complications from the operation. Only time will tell about the other. I hope for the best—not only for Mrs. Jernigan but for the procedure. You are well aware this type of surgery is in the experimental stage."

The family had risen, a kind of fortress behind their father. Jacob said, "Thank you, doctor. I've been praying to the great Physician to guide your hand. He's brought us so far. I believe he will see us through."

"Amen!" Lily's voice resounded.

The doctor smiled broadly. "Thank you, Jacob." His tone was not condescending. He put one arm around Jacob's shoulder and addressed the family. "You know you have a remarkable father. It has been a rare privilege to get to know him. If the world were made up with just half of Jacob Jernigans, the other half would change overnight. I can't predict the future of your mother's health, but if faith, goodness, and trust have anything to do with her recovery, she's got it made." Once again he took Jacob's hand in both of his. "I'll be around and seeing you for the next few days."

Deborah dabbed at her eyes and stood aside as her four sisters took turns hugging their father. From the top floor of the hospital, she gazed down at the network of streets—many of them one-way—and pondered mazes. She felt like Daedalus, trapped in a labyrinth of her own building. She could not escape the echo of her mother's words and the awful guilt that accompanied it. She hoped with all her soul that Anna would not remember, and if she did, there would be no remorse. "I need a priest to hear my confession and give me absolution," she said to herself. "No absolution without belief," she whispered.

Jacob Jernigan put his arm around his daughter. "Give it time, De-Borah. Let God take care of it. In his own time he will."

"Time," she whispered back. But Dylan Thomas's words rang in her ears: "Time held me green and dying/Though I sang in my chains like the sea."

"Sister," Hannah said, addressing Deborah, "do you wonder how Mama might be changed after this?" Thoughts and remembrances, the compound of guilt, had etched premature lines in her face in her twenties after the death of Emily. Now she stood with her gnarled hand resting on Deborah's slender shoulder, a scarecrow draped in unmatched skirt and blouse, her voice dry as corn shucks rustled by dry winds.

"What do you mean, Hannah? What kind of change?"

"Will she remember?"

"I don't know how much of the past will be blotted out. The parts that hurt, I hope."

"Reckon they'll start giving lobotomies? Like a prescription, maybe?" Not even a tear softened her dull eye.

"If they do, Hannah, let's have one together," Deborah whispered as she took her hand to lead her to an easy chair.

"Well, praise the Lord!" It was Lily, who stood facing her siblings, although she was looking directly at Deborah, the Jernigan infidel. "I think we all ought to get down on our knees right here and thank Jesus."

"Not here, Lily. The chapel on the first floor would be more appropriate. Besides this is a public room," Deborah said as her eyes surveyed other groups awaiting news of relatives.

"I'm not ashamed to acknowledge my Savior anywhere," Lily retorted. She was like a Druid goddess gowned in pristine white accentuating a robust figure curved only by the staves laced tight around the waist. Minus a pulpit, she affirmed her faith loudly. Anger reddened her otherwise pale face devoid of makeup.

Jacob rose slowly. "Let's all go to the chapel. We all need to stretch our legs," said the peacemaker without the usual "Tut, tut." Beckoning his youngest child to his side, he led the Jernigan clan to the door.

"No doubt who rules the roost in this family," Lily muttered.

"Hush!" Beryl whispered.

CHAPTER

Twenty-Two

RESPITE, RESPITE, AND NEPENTHE

———————————————

"It was the best of times; it was the worst of times." So said Dickens in Victorian England where rampant crime, unjust punishment, and empty larders plagued the poor; while others, safe behind ancient thick walls built by slave labor, enjoyed God's bounty—chocolates, truffles, and vintage wine—as they reclined on velvet in salons, half-listening to chamber music. Such was the typical lecture of Miss Jernigan standing in front of her English class.

"Can't you see fat old dowagers enveloped in mink looking down on the underlings of the world through bejeweled lorgnettes?" Miss Jernigan said mockingly.

The colorful language amused them though they could not muster the teacher's intense pity for the poor nor the scathing disdain for the unworthy. Perhaps they did spot the bitterness in her voice that sometime emerged whether the lesson was participles and split infinitives or Sophocles' *Oedipus Rex.* Sons and daughters of professionals whose worries did not include financing college or even a date for the Junior-Senior Prom could identify more easily with Dickens' "best of times" than his "worst of times."

Deborah knew her clientele and had the good sense not to applaud the Supreme Court decision on May 17, 1954, to integrate public schools. Yes, she was bitter about the Olivias of the world, black or white, who were trapped in poverty and humiliated by fathers addicted to the bottle and unable to buy a coffin to give wives decent burials—bitter that at twenty-five she also was trapped. Somehow the world of sleigh bells and real snow and red bicycles and impassioned kisses had eluded her. Red pencils, companions of the night, glided over student papers on which she struggled to temper criticism with praise. Weekends she spent at Mount Tabor with a mother still dazed but obsessed with time, insisting that all watches and clocks be synchronized with the Lady Elgin, a gift from the family, remembered only because it was a welcome home present. "Thanks for small things," Deborah said to herself. In addition to Anna's fixation with time, other aberrations wrought by the lobotomy had emerged. Severed frontal lobes no longer monitored her tongue and whatever passed through the brain found its way to her mouth, language alien to proper Southern speech—the kind that in the past sent children to soap and water to purify their mouths. Uninhibited speech matched her taste in gaudy clothes. To compensate for the past, Deborah indulged her mother in fancy dress. On her fiftieth anniversary Anna wore a pink lace dress at noon at a picnic spread on makeshift tables in the backyard. No one had any idea how many people to expect. Anna had invited guests via telephone but could not remember who or how many. Her hair tinted blue and finger-waved the day before, she appeared in her finery that fell flowingly to her bare feet. She was just as happy as if she were shod in satin pumps. Deborah smiled wryly and deigned not to answer when Belle demanded, "Deborah,

167

why didn't you get Mama proper clothes? Do you want us to be the laughing stock of the county?" Belle, however, was scandalized further when Anna responded to Uncle Thomas's opening remarks that intimated jestingly that Anna and Jacob had not always seen eye-to-eye and had fought vociferously as newlyweds. Anna retorted, "Tom, you're a black-faced liar!" Jacob's "tut-tut" curbed neither the laughter nor his wife's tongue. The youngest daughter laughed heartily, grateful for the diversion but envious that she, too, could not vent her spleen and find catharsis.

That school year Deborah actually had a proposal of marriage. A student's mother had invited the teacher to a dinner party where she was entertaining foreign soldiers from the nearby fort. Among them was a young Turk, who could quote Omar Khayam in Persian. On their third date Ilhan issued very formally a proposal of marriage, an obvious ploy, Deborah perceived, that would guarantee him citizenship in the land of plenty. Not even a kiss had preceded the offer. Despite the fact that she loved the *Rubayiat*—in English or Persian—she turned him down with, "You know, Ilhan, I would be great trouble in a harem. Besides, I'm a baptized Christian and a feminist. Also, I've never been much for praying, and I don't even know the direction of Mecca."

This conversation had transpired at a dinner party where the host dropped his wineglass on the white damask table cloth, and the hostess made a swift exit to the kitchen to stifle her laughter. So ended the possibility of giving her hand in wedlock. Later, Deborah wondered if the mother's uninhibited tongue had somehow loosened the daughter's.

In May came a telephone call from Stella, short of a doctorate in English except a dissertation.

"Deborah, I need you. I've just broken with Phillip. You know the math prof here at Ohio U. I can't bear him or Virginia Woolf right now. Go to Europe with me. I need my soul mate now. I'll finance it. Hush! You can pay me back. Besides, you need to get away. I even got special rates on plane fare. It won't cost that much. We'll hoof it with a book. Be our own tour guides. We can see how good our college French and Spanish are. Come on, Deb! Say yes!"

"God, Stell! I don't know. I need to be close to Daddy. He's been through a bad time. Besides, I need to save money to go back to school."

"You are not married to Jacob Jernigan. It's time you think of yourself. You'd be better off in a harem than stuck in Mount Tabor. Why didn't you marry Ilhan? At least you could see beyond the Low Country of South Carolina. Deborah Jernigan, you're in a nunnery. You might just as well shave your head and don a wimple."

Sitting at her desk grading the last term paper, she wrote the comment: *Fine effort yet the conclusion is illogical. The Dark Lady of the Sonnets most assuredly was not Queen Elizabeth. Besides, she had red hair.* Laughter joined the midnight chimes of the downstairs clock. She guessed what Stella would have written: "May I suggest you try Katherine of Aragon. She did have red hair." Stella had such a way with words. Deborah smiled, remembering the telephone call and wondered how long it had been since she really laughed. Stella could do that for her. Why not? She nibbled the blue uncut end of her marking pencil and stared unseeingly into space. Money. The summer checks would cover plane fare. She could borrow the rest. Snapping a rubber band around a mound of papers, she surveyed the room where she had lived for almost nine months. Frilly white organdy curtains draped a triple window and matched the bedspread on the French provincial bed. The room, now bringing rental income, had belonged to Mrs. Rivers' daughter, long married. White, white, white! Walls, carpet, furnishings—colorless, she thought. Exactly like my life. Stella is right, she mused. A whole world existed beyond this pristine room. Wordsworth's Lake Country—Keats' grave outside the city of Rome. What would it be like to take a gondola from St. Mark's Square in Venice? She could see Tim, still in the City of Lights, teaching seventeenth century English prose to French mademoiselles. Even the thought shook her with laughter. And

169

Francine—basking in the sun on the Riviera—just waiting for her American friend to visit. "I'm going," she said, stuffing her brief case. "Damn it! I don't care. And I won't even have a job when I come back. Maybe I shouldn't have resigned yesterday. But this place is too close to Mount Tabor. Well, I can always clerk in a dime store, but it's got to be close to the mountains. I'm sick to death of the Low Country! Sick to death of my life!" How quickly sobs had replaced mirth. She threw herself on the bed, clamped her eyes shut and began writing invisible notes. Passport—vacci-nation—cloth luggage to replace that heavy Samsonite, her gradu-ation gift. "Maybe I'll surprise Belle with a birthday gift," she muttered sleepily, remembering her sister's envy. Slipping into dreamland, she met John Donne, Dean of St. Paul's. He was lean-ing against a stone pillow and was quoting "To his Coy Mistress" in a voice remarkably like Tim Littlejohn's. Even in slumber she smiled.

She broke the news to Jacob and Anna together. "You are going to the old country?" That was Jacob's term for anywhere across the ocean. "Will you go where Jesus was born?"

"No, Daddy. England—Europe, the continent. Where our great-great-great-grandfathers and grandmothers came from. I'll get to know my English, Scotch, and Irish ancestry. I'll take lots of pictures; that is, if I can afford a camera."

"You ain't gonna fly?" There was fear in Anna's voice, remi-niscent of the old Anna before the lobotomy.

"No, Mama," Deborah lied. "Stella and I will be sailing on the Queen Mary—a five-day trip across the Atlantic. Don't worry. It's quite safe." She was not prone to prevaricate and would be caught in a lie when she wrote a postcard to them on the day the plane landed in London.

"How much will a camera cost, Deborah?" It was Jacob's question.

"Don't worry, Daddy. Stella will have one. I can always get duplicates."

On the morning that she boarded the Greyhound bus whose

170

destination was New York, Jacob handed his daughter a sealed envelope with her name written in his fancy cursive. "Open it later," he said as he kissed her cheek. Anna stood next to him. Not since the day when Anna had hurled those terrible words at her daughter had Deborah attempted an affectionate overture. Instead, she had lavished her with gifts—clothes which Anna in post-lobotomy character wore with a certain swagger. Today she was wearing a blue pillbox hat that matched her two-piece suit. On sudden impulse Deborah thrust her handbag into her father's hands and clasped her mother in a tight embrace. "I'll bring you something from Paris," she whispered as she kissed her on the cheek. Jacob smiled broadly. Deborah could almost hear his silent prayer of thanksgiving.

As the bus rolled away from the platform, she watched her mother's hand go up in a hearty wave. The white envelope lay on her black skirt. Inside, was a crisp fifty-dollar bill, fresh from the bank. A brief note. *Buy yourself a camera. I will pray for your safety. Love, Daddy.* The bus rounded the station and turned into the street. Through her tears she watched a gray-haired man with his arm around a woman in blue. She was still waving her hand goodbye as the two waited to cross to their parked car.

The next time Deborah cried was at the theatre in Stratford. The ticket agent had just told her and Stella that there were no seats available, not even standing room. "You mean we are not going to see a play? Not at any price?" It was a brilliant performance with a copious flow of tears—so effective that the lady pulled two sets from under the counter and said, "I was saving these for my cousins. But if it means that much to you, take them."

"Well, Miss Cornell," Stella laughed, "you have just been nominated for an Oscar."

Despite the fact that Stella had traveler's checks enough to finance a world tour, Deborah insisted they not go first or even second class. Pensiones in Italy, third-class hotels in Madrid, YWCA in Paris, private homes in England—humble abodes that enabled them to see first-hand middle class as well as view the magnificent edifices of bygone royalty. Adventures lay in wait around every corner. Mount Tabor, at times, no longer existed for its native daughter as the Jungfrau loomed in white gold or Michelangelo's breathing David silenced adulation. Their one indulgence was a prandial delight in a cuisine of note once a day. Wine accompanied their feasts and sometimes transported Deborah to a late afternoon brandy in a custard cup with a boy in overalls waltzing a girl in sawed-off jeans to "Moonlight and Roses" a cappella. The bittersweet memory warm as the vintage she sipped often conjured up the figure of Anna stealthily creeping into the smokehouse to sneak a snort of homemade brew fermented for medicinal purposes or marinade especially for Christmas fruitcake. Once she confided to her friend as she drained the last of the chardonnay, "Stella, if there is any truth in the tale that a mama can transfer her yen for brew to her unborn child, then I'm marked for life. Poor Mama! Living with a saint and concealing unholy longings. No wonder she had a breakdown. Her last born didn't contribute to her mental well-being either. You know, I threw the doll I got at Christmas in the fire—the doll that wore a miniature replica of her wedding dress that she had painstakingly fashioned for her baby daughter."

"Freud would have a heyday with you and your mama, my friend. Anyway, don't worry about becoming a sot. I'll rescue you from the nut house or skid row if I haven't joined you there myself." Her dark eyes studied the stem of the glass that she held. "You know, Deb, I dream about that baby. It was a boy." Drawing a circle with her glass on the table cloth, she continued. "Ted married a Miss South Carolina last month. The bastard! He didn't even send me an invitation. I was tempted to send him condoms for a wedding present. Maybe, though, his bride is a willing brood sow and will want to bestow upon him many little boys to carry on the illustrious Granville name." She raised her glass and proposed a toast. "Here's to us! The virgin and the whore." She smiled and added softly, "To the best friend I ever had."

Tired feet at the end of the day witnessed walking tours with books as guides. They communicated in classroom French and Spanish, accents that drew smiles from natives. When language failed them, they improvised. *Viva la France* was an improvised response for *Keep the change* along with dismissive hand gestures. A touch of romance in Rome brushed the two travelers as each of them had proposals by handsome Italian waiters who frankly admitted that their interests were not related to Eros but to Uncle Sam and American citizenship. Deborah especially found humor in the propositions. "Stella, do you suppose that my love life will always be attached to a passport?"

"Just wait until we meet Francine. That young doctoral candidate is just waiting to sweep you off your feet."

Francine and her brother, Jacques, shared an apartment in Cannes. A telephone conversation had finalized plans for a reunion. The good news was that Jean, who was completing his dissertation on Shakespeare, was visiting them. Stella was delighted with the prospect of her friend's meeting a Don Juan in love with iambic pentameter. "Do you relish a proposal in blank verse, Deborah?"

"Oh, I think I would prefer a villanelle."

"Deborah, this is Jean." There was a mischievous twinkle in Francine's eyes. Jean stood lean and tall, neatly tailored in casual clothes. He extended his dark brown hand to greet his blind date. "Jean is from the West Indies," Francine prattled on. "Don't worry, Jean. Deborah despises Jim Crow. Why, she led the march around the Capitol in South Carolina when the Supreme Court handed down its 1954 decision to ban segregation in the public schools." Now she scrutinized Deborah's reaction, devilishly testing her friend's professed liberal views.

As Deborah clasped Jean's hand, two thoughts bounced and collided: God in heaven, don't let me run into anyone from home. The other was even more earth-shaking. Can I dance with a black man? It was a moment of truth. What her mouth had espoused her Southern heritage was negating. The young man smiled graciously down at her. At once good sense prevailed. She clasped his hand firmly and said smilingly, "My word, Jean, what have you found new to say about the bard in your dissertation? "

"Nothing new." He flashed her a smile that traveled to his luminous brown eyes. "And I'm not focusing on black Othello and the white Desdemona. Nothing exciting, I'm afraid. A rather dull examination of textual differences in quartos."

They were on safe ground. Was there a moment of disappointment registered on Francine's face? Did she hope to sport her friend's consternation? Deborah smiled remembering the practical joker in good humor and admitted that she, too, was not above foisting discomfort on others. What followed was superb French cuisine prepared by her hostess peppered with sometime heated dinner talk. Stella, who was quite taken with Jacques, the brother, actually made tentative plans to meet him one weekend in Quebec, where he was currently studying forestry. Deborah couldn't help rolling her eyes and wondered how that arrangement if it materialized would set with the university boyfriend professor. Jean entertained with reviewing wild dissertation topics actually approved by the academic committee. One lad sought to prove that the animal imagery in *Macbeth* had the sole function to prove that Lord Macbeth was gay and that he murdered Duncan, not to achieve the crown but to get revenge because his former lover king had consorted with Macduff. Politics and the American racial problems escaped discussion, although both Deborah and Stella would have been ready to attest their views. The evening ended in Monte Carlo where the amateur gambler actually doubled a few French francs in the slot machine. Stella whispered, "What would Daddy Jacob say if he could see his daughter gambling with a black escort?"

Back in their hotel room Deborah queried, "How did I do, Stell?"

"Miss Cornell again. Nobody knowed you wuz a little gal from down South, where nigger men hang from trees and de women dos your laundry." They laughed companionably before slipping into dreamland. Deborah found herself back in Mount

174

Tabor at her parents' anniversary picnic and Anna pattering around barefoot in her pink waltz-length dress. Jean was nowhere in sight.

Three months in another world. Wordsworth's Tintern Abbey; flowers on Keats' grave ironically located across from Rome's garbage dump, ill-fitting for one who worshipped beauty; *Medea* in Spanish in an open-air theater in Madrid at midnight; a trip down the Rhine where the two in trivial argument missed the Lorelei; *Aida* in the ruins of the Baths of Caracalla with a cast of a thousand—these were sights when Deborah, sounding like a broken record, would turn to her friend with, "If this is a dream, don't wake me up." She was far from the black and white world of Mount Tabor. No better antithesis of that world was Paris, where they finally joined Tim on holiday from the Sorbonne.

They met by arrangement at a sidewalk café off the Place de la Concorde, a place Tim assured them had been Hemingway's and Fitzgerald's haunt. Stella knew Professor Littlejohn only through Deborah's letters, but even the sophisticate raised her eyebrows slightly when he was introduced.

"Stella, this is Tim." A baggy black sweater had replaced the double-breasted suit. A pewter ornament dangled from a leather cord around his neck. Even the hairstyle had changed. It was brushed to the front monk fashion, but most amazing was the goatee that sprang from the once small chin. The eyes were Tim—still big and brown and peering through gold-rimmed granny glasses. Beside him stood his companion, a fellow teacher. Philippe could appropriately be Mutt's Jeff. He stood over six feet tall in moccasins without socks. Shoulder-length blond hair parted in the middle framed a face chiseled in the likeness of a Donatello sculpture. Eyes, Mediterranean blue, smiled quizzically from unbelievably long lashes. Deborah toyed with the idea of cupping that chin and tracing the lines of the sensuous lips. Adonis in the flesh. He must have read her thoughts. In an accent she could not identify, he murmured, "I am already spoken for," and winked mischievously at Tim. Her cheeks flamed as

175

she groped for a smart retort. It was the ever resourceful Stella who quipped, "We are not shopping for sleeping companions. A fine French cuisine and perhaps some literate confab will do just fine."

"Touché, Mademoiselle. That you shall have."

It was another unforgettable experience, a respite indeed. A whole ocean separated her from essays inked in red and Mount Tabor in black and white. French cognac, this time not filched from the smokehouse behind Mama's jarred vegetables, and the soft twilight of a summer evening blurred visions of that other world. Even the light and dark figures performing the dance of life and death at the Folies Bergère burgeoned no sinister thoughts. Instead, Deborah Jernigan smiled as she contemplated the diversity of friends and the complex, though satisfying relationships, however ephemeral they might be. Late bonsoirs each night ended with warm embraces and actual tears at good-bye.

On that last night in the City of Lights just before sleep, Deborah whispered to Stella, "How long will it last? Philippe and Tim?"

"Deb, you are an odd mixture—incurably romantic and pessimistic. Carpe diem! Who knows about the morrow? My philosophy is grab what you can today. We have no assurance that there will be a tomorrow. In the morning you may be turned into a cockroach and worry about how you can facilitate turning over on your belly so that you can crawl."

"You sound like a Baptist evangelist who has just heard of existentialism."

"I'm too sleepy to philosophize." There followed a prolonged yawn. "What you need is a whammy of a love affair to put you on cloud nine before it knocks you down to earth again. Love ain't always made in heaven. Tim, Philippe, and I know that. Go to sleep and dream the impossible. It's as close as you will come to perfection on earth."

"I know, too," she thought. "But I wish—"

On a Sunday night Mount Tabor Baptist Church was packed

to see the slides from the "old country," as Jacob called his daughter's trip. Not one in the congregation had been overseas except veterans, who had not traveled abroad to look down on Swiss green slopes from Jungfrau or to light a candle in St. Peter's Basilica. It was an attentive audience. Even Anna was impressed and inquired how much one of "those mountain cabins would cost." She posed her question wistfully as she viewed a slide of a Swiss chateau and stirred September heat with a cardboard fan from Stewart's Funeral Home with a picture of the transfigured Jesus on the front. "Reckon you wouldn't need air-conditioning even in the summertime," she surmised.

"Deborah, Jesus never went to Rome or anywhere in Europe."

"No, Daddy, but Peter and Paul did. Both were executed there," she said as she flashed a picture of St. John Lateran.

"I wonder what Jesus would say about those magnificent churches built in his name. He mostly preached on a hillside or by a river."

Deborah's eyes caught her father's. "I wonder, too," she murmured softly.

CHAPTER

Twenty-Three

THE HANDMAID

J obless and broke, the European summer preserved in cellu-
loid, Deborah faced the possibility of free meals at the Jernigan table and substitute teaching at Union Grove. The prodi-
gal daughter, who had not even touched the fleshpots of Egypt,
had returned and the father welcomed her, but not so joyously as
he had in the past. Perhaps he, too, she thought, had succumbed
to the arid flatness of Mount Tabor. It withered in the summer's
drought, leaving fields of dried corn shucks standing like scare-
crows amid brown stubble. Eliot's lines rattled in her head. *This
is the way the world ends; this is the way the world ends; not with a
bang but a whimper.* A desert air rustled premature fall leaves, dead
without a hint of color. It was the autumn of discontent that had
wrought more than seasonal changes. A dry wind pervaded the
Jernigan household, bringing a kind of allergy that transformed
even Jacob's morning prayers before the breakfast table. His voice

had lost the timbre of humble thanks and fervent thanks. Deborah listened and noted the absence of crescendos which formerly accompanied his daily petitions and protestations of love to the Almighty. She wondered if her father had resorted unknowingly to the repetitive rituals of those whom he considered to be his apostate brethren, while his mind wandered to his wife, who had lapsed into a dream world of her youth.

Anna now had a litany all her own in which she recounted conquests of her girlhood, sometimes graphic enough to match modern day romances more daring than Lady Chatterley's lovers. Gone were her abilities to create a Southern cuisine in one pot with meat, vegetable, and bread. Her sporadic attempts to prepare a meal resulted in a charred tea kettle or the residue of the makings of boiled custard burned black on an eye of the range. Soap operas replaced housewifery and lathered the details of her imagined youth. Deborah, whose talents had never claimed expertise in cooking or cleaning, abandoned books for pots and pans as she assisted Jacob in the kitchen. Their combined efforts to prepare an edible dinner or supper were as uninspiring as the tales Anna concocted. Turnip greens and pork chops, collard greens and beef stew, turnip greens and stewed chicken—daily fare with leftovers for the pig pen, for neither Jacob nor Deborah was hungry while Anna ate without reflection on taste or variety. Instead, she lived with fantasies, but at odd moments she would finger the indentations at the base of her hairline and turn to her husband with "Jacob, how come you let them doctors bore a hole in my head? You think I was crazy?" Sometime her eyes focused on her daughter. "I bet a nickel you were behind it. You learned funny things at college, didn't you?"

Such remarks accompanied a fleeting gleam of hostility and an edge to her voice as she wrinkled her forehead as though she were searching for a missing link in her memory. At those times Deborah relived her own youth and watched the flames curl around the white dress on a princess doll and listened to her mother's imprecation, "I'd a been better off if you had never been

179

born." Baptized in guilt, she deliberated atonement. They needed her now, but if salvation meant staying in Mount Tabor, was it worth the price? Eliot's words reverberated: *Crucified upside down over an ant hill.* "I am no Cecilia," she said to herself. She reached for her mother's hand and met Jacob's eyes.

It was she who brought Ina to Jacob. One afternoon as they rocked together after supper on the front porch listening to the flutter of birds forsaking Mount Tabor for foreign climes, Deborah broached the subject. "Daddy, have you thought of getting someone to come in? I'm not much help, and we know Mama won't get any better. When I get to working again, I'll help with the expense. You need to get away. Besides, remember your heart condition. What about your church that means so much to you? You haven't left Mama since I have been here. She's not unhappy. You have to stop worrying about her so much. You have a life, too. Think about it, will you?" The words tumbled out. It was her desperate attempt to find escape for both of them.

His response startled her. "You're right. I need somebody. Especially after you leave." Deborah dared not look at him, but the break in his voice bespoke watery eyes gazing vacantly into the days ahead. She stretched one slender hand over his squat, calloused fingers splayed on his denim knee. "Remember when I used to ask when my fingers would get as big as yours?"

"You got pretty hands. Mine have seen hard work. Carpenter's hands. Maybe like our Lord's." The pressure in his clasp teared her eyes.

A week later Ina Curry came to live with them. Not since black Ginger, her childhood nurse, had there been a full-time servant at the Jernigans. Ina was white. She was the daughter of a sharecropper who farmed tobacco, cotton, and soybeans, the money crops in the Low Country. With the drought, it had been a bad year with scarcely enough return for labors to cover the cost of fertilizer for landowners or the necessary expenses for the mean livelihood of the tenants. The Currys were not of the number of ambitious sharecroppers who worked hard, grew their own vittles, and at the end of the year had incurred little debt so that the money crop was saved and eventually invested in their own farm. The Currys were the kind who preferred bologna sausage from the local commissary to the cured hams from their pigs. Store-bought clothes were more appealing than homemade ones from Singer sewing machines. Unlike many of their neighbors, the Currys spent their cash at the end of the season on second-hand cars and Saturday night trips to town and a bottle of cheap whiskey.

Ina was twenty-two. Two of her younger sisters were already mothers. Ina's education had been terminated in grammar school, since she showed more promise chopping cotton in the field than doing sums on tablet paper. Her looks were not responsible for her single marital state. In truth, though she could not boast of great beauty, she was not unattractive. A few clothes and a hair salon might have accomplished wonders. Her tall, lean figure curved in the right places. Brown hair with just a hint of a curl framed her tanned face devoid of makeup. Her eyes were her most remarkable feature. They were also brown, but big, kind, humble, and luminous eyes which she was prone to cast down when she was addressed. Occasionally, she stole sly glances that briefly glinted with laughter or with something else that Deborah could not define. Neither body nor facial impairment had marred her social life. The trouble was her speech. Ina stuttered. In mid-sentence she would wage battle with one syllable in futile effort to complete the sound until finally ending in a volley of words shot out like cannon. It was no wonder that she seldom spoke. One of her longest speeches came one afternoon when Deborah, whose size nine dresses fitted Ina, decided to share clothes from her wardrobe. The few faded but clean frocks that belonged to Ina brought back vivid memories of Olivia, the bright student whose dead mother lay in an airless room awaiting a charity coffin. As Ina smoothed a red tartan over her slender hips, she whispered, "You just like Mr. Jacob," she stammered, wrestling over the name. "Thank you."

Efficient in the house as well as in the fields, Ina scrubbed forgotten corners, turned out gleaming white linen including Jacob's Sunday shirts, and made apple strudel just the way they liked it. Working her magic and seldom speaking, she moved silently from room to room, a wraith-like figure that disappeared when she was not needed. Jacob and Deborah were pleased, but Anna at the outset registered disapproval. "How come you bring that girl in my house? Ain't said two words to me all day."

Jacob in his usual role as peacemaker replied, "It's all right, Mama. She's here to help out 'til you get better. The Lord has sent her to us."

"Humph! Ain't any good coming from her being here."

Deborah exchanged knowing glances with her father, smiled, and felt pleased. She had wrought a miracle that had brought some semblance of order and at the same time had delivered herself from bondage.

CHAPTER

Twenty-Four

NEW ACQUAINTANCES

I t was the good Lenora, who opened the gate to escape. There were no huckleberries to pick, and no fish in the dried up pond; but the two walked often through the brown woods. One afternoon Lenora came with a copy of *The State*. She had encircled in red a classified ad. *Wanted: English teacher for immediate employment in community college.* There was a number to call, an interview arranged, and a dossier submitted. With blessings on her lips for Lenora, Deborah Jernigan set out once again in her green vintage Buick, this time for Georgia.

The flat lands gave way to hills and black earth turned to red clay. The town stood on the banks of the Savannah River just a paddling boat away from South Carolina. Maryville boasted of the broadest downtown streets in the Southland with names as old as the signers of the Constitution. It was not the ideal assignment; yet it was not Mount Tabor and the waters of the Savannah

183

were plentiful enough to gush pleasantly against the shore on an autumn evening.

Determined to make the best of the situation, Deborah, a week late for work, entered the classroom. She soon found that teaching English O99 taxed not the brain but tested the patience. They had matriculated at the community college, many from the mills and farms in outlying areas. Their speech was a patois of Tara and the mid-fifties slang where "making-out" connoted heavy sex and "tough" a myriad of meanings among which transformed an inedible dish into a viand. The responsibility of the teacher, however, was not to train orators or speech writers but to work a miracle in one semester that magically produced a coherent essay, a passing grade, and entrance into college credit courses. The teacher who posted failures from over half of her charges was likely not to have a renewal of contract next spring. The Chairman of the Department, whose classes were the crème de la crème, shook his gray head as he perused her grades and even though his smile was benign and his manner avuncular, he said, "Deborah, we have to do something about this."

"We, Dr. Peters? Are you offering to assist me in turning sixty sows' ears into silk purses?"

"Well, I haven't heard that expression since I left the farm," he chuckled. "I think your aspirations are too high. Your students are not here to produce the polished word. Basic communication is what we are after. Forget parallel structure and consistency of metaphor. Sows' ears make up the stockyard of society and sometimes invade the professionals. I bet your doctor could not produce an essay that would come up to your expectations. Listen to your Sunday sermons. Platitudes and repetitions." His blue eyes twinkled. "Show these youngsters your human side. They are scared to death of you."

There was no getting around the truth. There was wisdom in his words. Somewhere she had lost her sense of humanity. She remembered that year at Tomahawk High where she had performed miracles. The trouble was that she was miserable. Each evening she went home to an upstairs one-bedroom apartment partitioned on the side of what was once an antebellum home. Neither the phone nor the doorbell rang. It was her fault. She had been elated to land a job in a college, and then she had been assigned remedial English classes. Her academic ego had been perforated. Jealous of colleagues who taught upper classes, she had developed paranoia and imagined their feeling superior. Now she had begun to doubt her capability. She had boxed herself into her misery. Unhappiness had perhaps translated to her associates a false hauteur.

As she mulled these thoughts alone with a second cup of tea made the English way, the ghost of Maureen appeared with a tripod and a camera and an overnight bag. Her weekend liaisons were an effort to penetrate her peculiar wall of loneliness. She is now "safe in her alabaster chamber," Deborah mused. But there was Jacob, her kind, gentle father, buttressed by a faith so impregnable that even a wife of over half a century who now lived in a twilight zone between sanity and madness could not shake his protective love. He had survived. "But I am Anna's daughter." She voiced these words to empty rooms. Was she also a candidate for tranquilizers and shock treatment? Shuddering, her fingers loosened their hold on the delicate handle of the blue Wedgwood cup she had bought last summer in England. The cup clattered in the saucer. There was no break, although the remnants of her tea splashed brown stains onto the linen weave of the placemat. At that moment the telephone rang.

"Deborah, this is Michael Peters. I have an extra ticket to the symphony tomorrow night. My wife, Elizabeth, is in Atlanta babysitting our grandchildren."

"How wonderful! I would love to go. What time?'

Eight o'clock the next evening found her ensconced in seat number thirteen in the township auditorium. Stella's gift from Paris, a red silk cape threaded in gold, draped her best black dress.

Turning to Dr. Peters, she chatted amiably, "Look! Poe would have called thirteen unlucky. I feel so lucky to be asked. 'Thank you, so much! I love music! Oh! And my favorite Beethoven! *The Pastorale!*" she added as she scanned the program.

"Mine, too," he answered warmly. "I'm sorry Elizabeth is missing Stokowski. What a treat to have him here. Maryville is not New York. Anyway, thank you for joining me."

Deborah smiled companionably and turned to acknowledge the lady who was just occupying seat fourteen. The newcomer nodded politely. Settling herself comfortably, she opened up her program. On impulse she murmured, echoing Dr. Peters, "What a treat to have Stokowski!"

Michael Peters leaned across his guest. "Frances, I want you to meet Deborah Jernigan. Deborah, this is Frances Waters. My wife and she both teach piano to children. On the most part, the youngsters are sent to them by mamas ambitious to turn their tone-deaf offsprings into Rubensteins. The two of you meet on common ground. Deborah here is trying to turn remedial English students into writers," he finished chuckling.

Deborah surveyed the woman beside her. *Regal* was the word. Even in her fifties she was beautiful. She wore in an upsweep—a crown of black curls feathered in gray. What was arresting were her eyes. They were dark brown and startlingly big. Talking eyes, Deborah thought, that did not need a mouth to communicate. Behind her smile there lurked a brooding sadness too painful, perhaps, to verbalize. When she spoke, Deborah decided she was sitting beside an Italian diva without the usual girth. It was a voice low and musical as if her words were strung together like notes after the treble clef.

It was a cordial but timorous greeting. Deborah had the distinct feeling that a door had cracked between her and this stranger, but it would be she, not Frances, who would need to promote entrance. Although she was not prone to overt gestures, she found her hand clasping the hand beside her.

The houselights lowered and darkened. Into the pit came the great man as the auditorium shook with applause. One of the rea-

sons Deborah had been excited about getting a job in this Georgia town was the wide cultural activities it offered. Now as the soft
strains of Beethoven flowed from the maestro's bow, she repeated
last summer's trip down the Rhine, past the Lorelei, Bonn, the
castles on the hill, the sheep grazing on the green slopes. She
turned to her companion whose eyes were closed and who perhaps was creating her own landscapes. It was the beginning of a
deep and abiding friendship, one that would stretch through the
years with mirth and pain.

As the last notes of *The Moldau* closed the program, Deborah
turned to her new acquaintance. "Smetana does with notes what
I used to try with words. But I'm neither a poet nor Prince Hamlet," she said paraphrasing Eliot.

"I try to write poetry, but most of the time I am Prufrock,"
demonstrating her familiarity with Eliot.

"In college I tried my hand in verse. What I wrote was not
poetry—more like doggerel—maybe not quite that bad. I would be
ashamed to show it to anyone. I think I could handle prose better.
I would like to write a novel some day. Right now all I have time
to do is to write comments on student papers. I'd love to read
some of your poems though.

Stokowski had returned to the podium for an encore, Gersh-
win's "I've Got Plenty of Nothing." As the maestro's animated baton crashed the last notes, Frances Waters leaned over, speaking
above thunderous clapping. "Bob and I are having a few friends
over for steaks Saturday night. Can you come?"

Bob Waters, a rotund Southern gentleman, was twenty years
older than his wife. On Saturday evening he lifted his glass of
Jack Daniel to his guests with, "Here's to us gentlemen. There
ain't many of us left." His portrait hung over a Hepplewhite sofa.
Despite the glowing cigar in his hand, the artist had captured a
demeanor belonging to a stern judge about to administer justice,
a striking contrast to the genial figure of the short bald man now
robed in his chef's apron, apparel for frequent cookouts in his
backyard. This staunch segregationist who published weekly dia-

tribes of states' rights and "separate but equal schools" had for years been called the "kingmaker" for any aspirant to the governor's office or to a senate seat. Over the mantel on the opposite wall Frances Waters faced her husband. It was the portrait of a young woman whose dark curls hung shoulder-length. She wore a low-cut burgundy gown softly edged with frills. If the dark eyes which followed you wherever you stood in the spacious room had cared to speak, they might have revealed dark secrets.

Across the room on a raised platform stood a baby grand Steinway where Frances now sat. Her fingers caressed the notes of a Chopin etude, and then as almost suddenly aware of a cocktail party, her hands moved swiftly into "St. Louis Woman." Some of her guests began swaying to the rhythm.

"It doesn't quite fit, does it?" he commented. The words came from a tall man with receding blond hair perhaps in his mid-fifties. As Deborah looked up into his blue eyes, she felt small, not that she just came to his shoulders, but that she somehow felt insignificant. The quality of the voice was low in the bass register and invited no answer. A strange sensation seized her. This man who stood leaning against the piano could read her thoughts, a knowledge both exciting and frightening.

"Have you known them long?" she ventured.

"Oh, yes! Bob Waters is quite a fellow. He grows camellias and can cry like a baby in sympathy. Many faces has our Bob. I remember once when the brakes gave way on his driveway just after we had made a trip to replenish his liquor supply at a New Year's Eve party that he braked with his foot out the open door until the car stopped on level pavement. You ought to see him in the courtroom. Once he got into a tussle with a prominent citizen in this town. The two rolled under one of the benches in the courtroom."

"But Frances. His wife. How did they ever get together?"

"He married her," he chuckled. "Don't underestimate his beautiful lady. There's more than just poetry and music." He reached for her empty glass, his fingers lightly brushing hers.

"Only after the second drink can you enjoy the human menagerie."

"Well, doctor, I hear you giving them boys in med school hell. They scared to death of you." The speaker was a short man with red hair and a healthy girth. Puffy bags under glassy eyes bespoke many nights with John Barleycorn. His eyes slid over Deborah's red velvet cocktail dress.

"Charlie, let the young lady alone. She's new here. Besides, your wife is watching you."

He had not even asked what she was drinking. Returning, he handed her the glass. "Bob pours them healthy. 'An ounce of civet to sweeten your imagination.'"

"Imagine a doctor quoting *Lear!*"

"This evening is full of incongruities."

"Well, I see you have already met." Frances Waters had abandoned the piano to join them. "Deborah, this is Lance Addison. Despite his specialty in medicine, he quotes like a Bartlett. Lance, Deborah teaches at the college—English. Why don't we three go into the kitchen? You can help me with hors d'oeuvres."

By that time many had drifted out into the backyard. Lance seated himself at the large table centering the kitchen and motioned Deborah to join him. Nearby, Frances emptied nuts into wooden bowls. "When Frances invites you here, you have entered the inner sanctum," he said. "More tales have been told, more scandals unveiled, including my own, than in any other spot in Maryville except perhaps the confessional at Saint Joseph's."

"Deborah, this is where I do my writing when I try to write."

"Here she translates what she hears at night around this table into metaphor, a language not for the common herd." His head nodded toward the voices coming from the other room.

Deborah took a deep breath and sipped her drink, hoping that it would calm her heart. There was no wedding ring on his left hand. He wore only a large college ring marked *MD*. Again he read her.

189

"Divorced. Bob Waters delivered me from the clutches of Circe and has freed me forever from nuptial bonds. But not from love," he added playfully.

"Lance Addison, stop it!" Frances ordered. Don't let his poetic tongue beguile you. Lance is short for Lancelot."

"Well, I'm not Guinevere, Frances. Don't worry."

"Maybe you're the Lady of Shallot. Maybe you need to come down from your ivory tower. I even have a small boat we might launch out in one of these nights." There was an amused twinkle in his eyes.

"Before I come down, I would have to like what I see below," she returned. Frances looked up from the salad tray she was assembling and shook her head.

"Touché, Deborah. You know for years I pronounced that Bible name De'borah. Not even my Sunday school teachers knew any better. Wasn't your namesake somebody important?" he asked. "I bet somebody has called you De'borah."

"My father did, and Deborah was a judge in Israel." Her hand tightened around the now-empty glass. She was remembering the time when she was quite little and going to Pawley's Island with her father. When her feet first hit the sandy shore, she felt as though she was moving with the waves that lapped her bare feet. She would dig her toes into the sand to steady her, but then there was always Jacob's strong hand as he led his daughter into deeper and higher waves. Now she felt that same surge, the pull of the tide, but tonight there was no hand to catch on for support.

"Miss Deborah, you are about to taste the finest steaks this side of the Great Pee Dee River. Bob Waters stood in the kitchen doorway laden with a trencher of charcoal cooked T-bones. "Few whites and no coloreds eat like this."

Hours later, Deborah lay stretched out in her bed staring into the darkness. She tried to recall names and match them with faces around the dining table. She could get no further than her host and hostess before Lance Addison's devilish twinkle flashed. Frances' words came back to her as they stacked the dishwasher after dinner. "It's none of my business, Deborah, but I just want you to be careful. Lance Addison is too old for you. He's old enough to be your father. Don't mistake him for one."

What did she know about Lance and why then had she paired them as a couple for a dinner party? Had the possibility that meeting him would have consequences not occurred to her? Tonight she had observed what was happening. An inexperienced, naïve little teacher from the Low Country had gone cuckoo over a middle-aged doctor who could quote Shakespeare as glibly as he could announce interest in an affair but not marriage. The scoundrel had read her thoughts. Well, that was the end of that. Frances need not worry. He had left after dinner without even a polite "I'm glad to have met you."

She had drunk too much. Alcohol, as Jacob would say, had wrought its evil. "The abomination in the sight of God" had turned her into putty and made her transparent to a stranger. Her face burned with embarrassment. The little girl who had drunk cognac prom night on her front porch with her high school friend had had more sense than the twenty-six year old that now lay tossing sleeplessly.

The phone on the night table pealed twice before she found it. "Daddy?" Who else would be calling at two on Sunday morning?

"Lance. Do you go a godding on Sunday or would you prefer breakfast around noon and a ride out to Clarks Hill. I hear the fish are biting, but I'm not the compleat angler. I leave that to Isaac Walton. I just thought you might like to watch the crappies jump."

"What's all this crap about at this hour? Are you trying to flaunt your knowledge of a survey course in English literature and at the same time ridicule good churchgoing people.?"

"No, I'm fishing for a string of clever rebuttals from a smart mouth English teacher who surfed last night batting her brown eyes in a catching fashion."

"Do fish have brown eyes? If they don't Dr. Addison, you

have just mixed a metaphor."

"I think I need a refresher course. You see I flunked English 101. A free breakfast and ride. Wouldn't that be an acceptable fee for a tutor? I promise to treat my teacher with the greatest respect and have her home before dark. But you know the lake is kind of nice with the fish flapping on gold water at sunset."

"Would you think me easy bait if I accept?"

"No, I would think myself lucky to have reeled in a charming companion for a few hours." There was nothing flip about his response. Instead, the words came soft and low with unexpected sincerity.

"Just don't throw me in. I'm not a good swimmer. Promise?"

"I promise."

CHAPTER

Twenty-Five

THE TIGER EYE

They were sitting in folding chairs in a secluded spot by the lake. It was one of those warm afternoons—springtime in early winter—with the thermometer hovering around eighty. To Deborah the intermittent lap of miniature waves echoed the ebb and flow of Wagner's Love-Death theme from *Tristan and Isolde*. She had just recounted the tale of her first grade classroom and Miss Agatha's board of education.

"Well, we have something in common. You got the paddling for spelling words, and I lost a spelling contest," Lance chuckled. "Maybe we ought to stay away from words. They seem to be our enemies."

Moments passed. Each stared out across the pewter expanse of water where a boat bearing a lone figure sat motionless. His right hand reached for hers and brought it to rest on his knee. The index finger polished the tiger eye in the silver ring she was wearing.

"Tell me about losing the spelling contest."

"I like your ring. It's supposed to have healing powers. Everything from high blood pressure to depression. An old Indian told me it gives confidence and courage. The Roman soldiers wore it for protection in battle. They say if you look at it in sunlight, you will be able to look into the future. Which of the reasons are you wearing it, Deborah?" he asked quizzically.

"Maybe all of them, but I had no idea it had such super powers. I bought it in a little shop in Asheville, North Carolina. I was celebrating passing my orals for my degree. I should get one for my mother. She's been depressed as long as I can remember. Right now she's in another phase. Maybe a little mad. Anyway, get back to the spelling contest."

"I bet your tiger eye came from quartz mined in the Blue Ridge Mountains. I was born in them thar hills. Your stone has a nice yellow luster." He laced his smooth tapered fingers through hers.

They were not like Jacob's stubby calloused ones. Jacob's touch didn't do odd things with her heartbeat. Undoubtedly a doctor could spot a racing pulse easily. Drawing her hand away, she said, "Aren't you going to tell me about the spelling contest?"

"'Tiger, tiger, burning bright in the forest of the night,' he chanted. I wonder if William Blake ever saw a tiger eye."

"The spelling contest," she repeated.

"Persistent, aren't you? I was just a little boy in knickers representing my school in the county spelling bee. The word was *chauffeur*. The official accented the first syllable. So I spelled it *shofar*. Of course, the little town girl gave it the French spelling. 'No, no, sir! It's what the Jews blow. The horn. It's in the Bible.' My protest fell on ignorant ears. 'Not fair!' I whimpered. My mother hurried me out before I made a bigger fool of myself."

"Oh, Lance! How sad!" This time her hand clasped his. He leaned over and kissed her lightly on the lips.

The sun had just spilled into the lake where it shimmered around the boat painted on a gold background. "Look at your tiger eye. The sun fadeth. 'Tis your last chance to read the future," he teased.

"I don't want to look. Today is enough."

"Today is never enough, my dear. We mortals may think we can live by the moment and take no thought of tomorrow. I think that was the advice Jesus gave his disciples. Look where they ended up. They all lost their heads," he chortled.

"I'm not losing mine, Lance. I know what is happening. No tiger eye has to tell me. I'm—"

He drew her to her feet and stopped her words with firm fingertips on her lips. "What is happening is that I am about to kiss a girl who has eyes as brown as the tiger's. It's the only way I can stop her from talking."

It was a long, deep kiss. The world around her shrank into the narrow enclosure of his strong arms. The sun stood still, and old Joshua was nowhere around.

"The tiger is warning you. Do you like his 'awful symmetry?'" he whispered, as he looked at her intently, his hand cupping her chin.

"I am scared, Lance. Let's go. Now!" she commanded. "It's getting late."

"All right," he said. "It may already be too late." He took her hand to steady her and led her silently through a forest of trees to the car. Opening the door, he said, "Your tiger eye has spoken, hasn't he?" He searched for her lips and found only her cheek. As he turned the key in the ignition, she groped for a verbal riposte that would put her on firmer ground. She knew that words were dangerous. It was safer to say nothing.

◆ ◆ ◆

Dear Stella.

At last it has happened. There is a man in my life—at least there was one this afternoon. Lance Addison is mid-fifties, a doctor and divorced

195

who announces interest in amours without com-
mitments. How shall I describe him? Tall, blond,
well-built but not portly—maybe not handsome
but appealingly masculine. I love his voice—soft,
low—almost musical—a voice just right to whisper
sweet nothings except he's too busy with clever
repartee sprinkled with literary allusions. He has
read widely and can demonstrate the breadth of
his expertise from quoting the Bard to unraveling
the mystical powers of the lowly tiger eye, the stone
in my ring. Stella, I am both charmed and fright-
ened and have the uncanny feeling that this man
can read my thoughts even before I have formalized
them. He knows that I have so easily succumbed
to his charm and intellect, and he may be amusing
himself with a naïve conquest. Yet this afternoon I
glimpsed a crack in a smooth façade that revealed
gentleness and tenderness in someone who under-
stands hurt.

Am I ready for a relationship on such terms?
An affair will not be easy for me with my Calvinis-
tic background despite my intellectual enlightenment. What would Jacob say? Is my attraction to
Lance Addison an unconscious replacement of my
sainted puritanical father with an older man both
uninhibited and world-wise? Lance says that medi-
tating in sunlight on the tiger eye can reveal the
future. At the moment I am truly in the dark.

Love,
Deborah

She folded the letter and eased it into the addressed envelope and jumped at the first ring of
the telephone. A soft, melodious voice murmured,
"Hello."

CHAPTER

Twenty - Six

"APRIL IS THE CRUELEST MONTH"

Winter in Maryville had been unnaturally mild with Jack Frost sparing many of last season's summer flowers. In the Waters' backyard, lush green Boston ferns hung leisurely from the eaves, untouched by the "blond assassin" and now the home of nesting birds. Long leaf pines splayed by a western sun danced in shadows over the lawn which was brilliantly encased in banked azaleas. Centering the verdant expanse, a dogwood bragged about her white Easter clothes to a blue sky. Against the English stucco house leaned a giant linden tree, newly leafed and ready for blossoms. Its fragrance would attract in May swarms of bees, thirsty for its nectar.

Bob Waters and Lance Addison watched the fire leap from the barbecue pit built against the brick wall. They each held a glass of Kentucky bourbon recently replenished from the makeshift bar on the wrought iron table topped with a slab of marble.

From their lawn chairs near the picnic table neither Frances nor Deborah could discern the import of their conversation, but Bob's frequent chuckle bespoke their good cheer. "It won't be long before the bees arrive," Frances said. "Deborah, it's a sight to see. They are such topers. They fall to the ground in drunken stupors. They ought to be a lesson to us," she laughed, lifting her empty wine glass.

"Nature is a great teacher," Deborah commented. "Unfortunately, we mortals don't listen." One hand swept the compass of the backyard. "Look at what's around us. Have you ever seen such glorious color? Yet Eliot says 'April is the cruelest month.' In a few weeks the flowers will be gone. There's nothing uglier than limp azalea blossoms strewn on the ground in wet deadness. Nothing lasts. Not even love—or what we think of as love."

"You think it's love, Deborah? What you and Lance have found?" She gazed vacantly into the tall pine tops. "I just hope you won't be hurt too badly. I feel kind of responsible. I'm the one who introduced you."

"You sound as skeptical as I am. Of course, I'll be hurt. What woman isn't vulnerable? Love?" She laughed. "Who dares define it? The poets do. They're drunk with metaphor. And there are the tragic operas and the dying divas. With their last breath they trill amour in high C's. Even sanctimonious Saint Paul, who warned 'it's better to marry than to burn,' and don't forget how hard he was on us women—he says, 'Love is without fear,'" she added cryptically. "But I suppose Paul was talking about spiritual love—the kind preachers harp on every Sunday."

"Speaking of preachers, have you mentioned Lance to your father?"

"You got to be kidding. I was home last weekend. Daddy and I didn't get around to talking. Don't misunderstand me. I wouldn't dare tell him that his baby daughter, his favorite child, the miracle that God wrought, was having an affair with a divorced man who has no intention of making her an honest woman. Lenore and

Beryl know, but they love me regardless of what I do. Anyway it may be my imagination, but I felt Daddy avoided me. I know he worries about what is ahead for Mama and him. It must be pretty dismal living with a mentally ill wife. Not much fun around. You know his world is black and white. Even a thought in color is sinful. And poor Mama! She doesn't like Ina at all. You would think that she would be grateful to have a good cook and somebody to keep the house spic and span. Ina frees her to immerse herself in soaps. I'm so glad Daddy is relieved of the chores. You know, I think he's genuinely fond of Ina. Mama is downright rude to her. My Mama is something else!"

"Frances, the coals are just about ready. You'd better check on what's cooking in the house. I'll go fetch the steaks." Bob Waters placed his glass on the nearby table. He drew out his pocket handkerchief and mopped his bald head glistening with sweat. "Hot damn! I can build a fire hotter than Lazarus' Hades." He smiled jovially. "Miss Deborah, it won't be long before I have the steaks on the table. I just turn them once. The red coals do the rest. By jingoes they come out good enough to make you want to whip your grand paw."

"How about your grand maw, Bob? Don't women need a little lashing now and then?" Lance teased, winking at Deborah, who bristled at his words. The chef's answer was lost as he followed his wife into the house.

"How goes it with thee?" Lance asked as he sat down beside her. "Still want to take a jaunt up to the mountains this weekend? I know a nice little motel right off the parkway. The view is nice." His arm dropped affectionately around her shoulder.

Deborah rose abruptly and made her way to the bar. As she refilled her wine glass, she answered. "I'm not going, Lance. I'm already behind with my papers. I'm sure you can get a substitute for me easy enough." The words were rushed and came unexpected even to her. "It's over, Lance."

"What's the matter? You're a regular little pasteurella pestis this evening."

"I'm just tired of being a whore." She looked at him squarely to ascertain the effect. His grin maddened her. She lashed out, "Stop patronizing me by using those damn medical terms. Incidentally, I do know what *pasteurella pestis* means. I'm not a bacillus. I don't see any signs of bubonic plague in you. I've given you nothing for the last five months except free meals and free bed pleasure." Her voice leaped across the peaceful stillness of the early spring evening.

"Don't be vulgar, Deborah. It's unbecoming. It's not like you." His manner was that of a parent mildly reprimanding an impetuous child. His indulgent smile refueled her anger. She sought desperately for venom potent enough to puncture his infuriating composure.

Before she could answer, Frances called from the back door. "Deborah, telephone. Your sister Beryl is on the phone."

Minutes later, Deborah replaced the telephone and turned to the trio hovering close. "Daddy is gone. Jacob Jernigan, my father, is dead." The announcement was formal and measured, words strung together on the same scale like dry clods of earth falling on lead. "Mama shot him. She says she caught him sleeping with Ina, our housekeeper."

Lance moved forward. He stretched out his arms to hold her. "Don't touch me, Lance. At last Jacob and his daughter meet on common ground—an adulterer and a slut." She dropped her head in her hands and heaved a dry sob. Raising her tearless face, she whispered, "'He was more sinned against than sinning.'"

CHAPTER

Twenty-Seven

RESURRECTION

They were there, her brothers and sisters, the children of Jacob. Death had stopped their bickering; death had humbled them. At last they were in one accord around the casket designed after the Order of Masons with four columns representing Solomon's Temple. Only Anna, his wife was missing. Valium had tranquilized her. She lay asleep under the multicolored quilt, her daughter's graduation present. The slumber seemed peaceful. Deborah prayed fervently. "If God will, let her upon waking, remember nothing."

William, the older son, now the patriarch of the family, had been the first on the scene. Outside his parents' house he had heard his mother scream. It was he who wrested the rifle from her clenched hands. The authorities had been kind, calling it an accident. Everybody knew that Anna Jernigan had had brain surgery. She was no longer a responsible person. Harry Stone, the sheriff, had listened politely as Anna gave a graphic account of her husband's bedroom folly. William had told his brother Mason that his mother had been retelling something she had seen on television. The family had concurred, supporting their brother's story. Only Deborah had said nothing. She had eyed Ina, who was prone to silence. Now she remained mute to questions. She simply stared into space, a comatose figure with eyes twin pools of grief. Deborah chose not to prod her. The rest of the Jernigan clan preferred to disbelieve their mad mother's tale rather than to accept the possibility of their sainted father's indiscretion. Deborah, however, relived last weekend's visit and recalled vividly Anna's open hostility to Ina. She had not cornered her father to question the state of affairs. In truth, she had been embroiled in her own dilemma as she faced the hopelessness of her own situation. Lance had not even once mentioned the word *love*, much less a suggestion of making their relationship permanent. Her practical mind urged an end of the affair; her heart told a different story. And so, her father's preoccupation had relieved her of the fear that he could spot his daughter's inner turmoil. Did he like her have a buried secret which would be revealed by an irate wife holding a 22 rifle and who, like Cassandra, nobody would believe? If he had found release, however temporary, in Ina's arms, his daughter found it good. Although she had suffered at the hands of his rigid theology, it had not even occurred to her to accuse him of hypocrisy. The words of her father's God came back: "Who among you without sin, let him throw the first stone." She found a kind of comfort in thinking that he, after all, had feet of clay—that his fall from his imposed exile in stern obedience to Jehovah's command had humanized him, had put him on the level of his beloved child. Yet she knew the consequence of that lapse, the lapse had he lived. A yellow-eyed tiger had emerged from a virgin forest on a warm afternoon in autumn and had warned her. She had turned a deaf ear.

Lenora's hands touched her shoulders. "Deborah, your friends are here, Stella and Dr. Addison. They want to speak to you before the funeral."

"Not now. I have to be with Daddy alone. They promised me a few minutes."

The lid of the coffin was closed for the last time. At last she was alone in the heavy-draped parlor. Cold glints of orange sunshine filtered through the open Venetian blinds casting psychedelic shadows on the mahogany box with the head turned toward the west. The three white lilies centering the cross had dropped their trumpets succumbing to the suffocating sweetness of massive banks of flowers in an airless room. Beyond the closed door, the mumbo jumbo of voices chanted the ritual of final arrangements. She had begged for this moment, and since she had refused to look at him or cry, her plea had been granted, though not without muted whispers behind her back. They were more curious about the living than the mystery of death.

She wished that she could cry, but her tears had dried up behind burning lids like parts of the Dead Sea. Behind those eyes lay scrolls of memory, but now they were an unassembled jigsaw puzzle. What she must do was to arrange the pieces in an orderly pattern.

Once upon a time a man was born in a small country village called Mount Tabor. He was this son of a carpenter who was a devout defender of the faith. This man was to follow in his father's footsteps adding to his tradesman's skills the tilling of the soil. Like his father he would be fruitful and multiply and would beget sons and daughters whom he brought up in the faith. He admonished them to abstain from worldly allurements and to pursue the way of righteousness. He was a good man. He gave generously to the poor and at the same time rendered his tithes to the storehouse in accordance with the scripture. He was rewarded with bountiful harvests which enabled him to enlarge his landholdings. Such was the accumulation of goods that he sent his daughter to houses of higher learning even though she would be taught alien doctrine. He had been proud of her although she had not accepted his faith. He had loved her. Now at three score years and ten he had died at the hands of a mentally unstable wife whom he had also loved and protected for over fifty years.

In addition to being a tiller of the soil, he had become the tiller of souls, and this son of a carpenter built chapels wherein he gave forth the sacred Word, a gospel written in black and white which he willed his children to accept. All had acquiesced except the daughter whom he had steadfastly defended even in her cruelty to her mother. Not once had he ever struck her. Instead, he had allowed her to whip herself—self-flagellation where the stripes are cut not on the body but on the soul. She had tilled a different field, a field of ideas planted by such minds as Schopenhauer, Nietzsche, Dostoevsky, and Kant. She had worshipped at the shrine of the great writers of the past and had found beauty not present at her father's altar. Instead she had denied his God. Now she could see the whole layout. The pieces of the puzzle were in place except for one.

Suddenly her shoulders shook with convulsive ragged sobs. "Daddy, wherever you are, forgive me. I tried so hard to believe, and now I do believe because I cannot accept your nothingness. Your love, your goodness, your humanity live on." The picture was complete.

A hand closed on her shoulder. It was Lance's hand. "It's time, my love. May I walk with you?"

With eyes brimful she said, "Thank you."

And with his arm around her, she followed her father's casket and listened to the words intoned: "I am the resurrection and the life."

To order copies of *Jacob's Daughter* as well as other titles
from Harbor House, visit our Web site:

www.harborhousebooks.com